"I'm not drunk, Nicola— I only wish I were!"

Drew gripped her arm, his accusing eyes moving from her tangled mass of hair to the bare expanse of skin she was vainly trying to cover up. "Now what the hell are you doing in that condition, at this time of night and in Redfern's room?"

Nicola struggled to escape. "You must be mad to speak to me that way," she gasped, staring into his scowling face. "I'm perfectly innocent!"

"Well, my cool and remote ice maiden, you're certainly out of character tonight. And here I thought you were so virtuous!" He pulled her tightly against his chest, so close she couldn't move. "But if this is a free-for-all, I might as well take my share!"

Land of Tomorrow

by

MONS DAVESON

Harlequin Books

TORONTO • LONDON • LOS ANGELES • AMSTERDAM
SYDNEY • HAMBURG • PARIS • STOCKHOLM • ATHENS • TOKYO

Original hardcover edition published in 1980
by Mills & Boon Limited

ISBN 0-373-02461-4

Harlequin edition published March 1982

CHAPTER ONE

THE river was wide, the further bank a long way off. She stood on the hot, dusty planks of the barge, her feet carefully avoiding the bubbling tar seeping through the cracks.

Brown water seethed in eddies and currents that a tide on the full was sending against the cumbersome vessel. Memories of other times she had travelled this waterway came crowding while the barge crept without any visible signs of progress along the thick hawser that appeared from beneath the water. Only the sound of its engine disturbed the mid-morning bushland stillness.

She must have been about eight years old all those years ago, she thought, and the barge in her memory was not so big and modern as this one. A voice interrupted her reverie.

'Nearly there, Miss Grant.' It was Mr Torrens who spoke from just beside her.

Nicola turned her gaze from the river. Slim, almost thin, medium height, her blonde hair swinging against shoulders held straight as if to announce to the world an ability to safeguard her own. Blue eyes swung up

5

to his face as his hand tapped her shoulder; he was continuing.

'Would you like to hop in, then we'll be off straight away when she grounds.'

Smiling acceptance, she put her hand in the owner of the barge's large one, to be helped up the steps into his Land Rover. 'This place is almost as out of touch as the back of beyond, isn't it?' she asked, taking her seat in the corner of the cabin.

'Yes,' the answer came back, 'but with this baby here,' he patted the shining bonnet of the big heavy vehicle, 'the back of beyond takes on the semblance of a comfortable black-top.'

Squeezed in between the ample, friendly, form of Mr Torrens and a stout tourist from, he said, far away Tasmania, Nicola hung on as the lumbering vehicle manoeuvred along two long planks on to a muddy track. For track was what it was! Teewah, their destination, was no developed resort, even this many years away from her childhood.

'The bank manager told me, Mr Torrens,' she interrogated her driver, 'that Teewah is still in a primitive state. He also said that beside some fishing shacks there's a new establishment being built. Do you know anything about it?'

'Too right I do. It's nearly finished. Catering mostly for fishermen, it's opening in a couple of days, I hear. I've heard too,' the words came dryly, 'that it's exclusive ... and expensive!'

Almost word for word what her bank manager had

concluded when explaining her father's estate, Nicola remembered. 'Your dwelling is only a shack,' he had gone on to say, 'but the land could become very valuable, being directly situated on the sea-front.'

'It's hard to believe,' she retorted now to her driver. 'A mere fishing camp—for smelly fishermen, exclusive ... expensive ... you must be joking!' She spoke with a laugh in her voice, happy somehow, because this expedition, which she had expected to be just an unpleasant chore to check upon her inheritance before putting it on the market, was turning into quite a picnic outing. She did tack on, however, 'Teewah does have big fish, though. I can remember my father catching them ... oh, so long ago.'

The converted coach bounced along the bush track, while Nicola gazed through the wide windshield before her. She found the countryside carried a memory —straggly bushland, scrub country. Nevertheless, coloured with thousand upon thousand of red candle-like tufts that pulsed and glowed among the drab grey-green, it held an attraction all its own.

'They make a show, don't they?' she asked, but continued before she could be answered. 'I also remember the wildflowers, but I realise it's not the season for them.' She wouldn't be here to see them, either, she knew. She was here only to inspect and then get out. Too many years had passed into the mists of time for her to have any roots here.

The heavy Rover lumbered on, a squeal or two issuing from the passengers in the back as they careered across two frail-seeming planks placed over a wash-away. Nicola glanced swiftly across at Mr Torrens. He merely grinned back complacently. This, then, she surmised, was only an added thrill for tourists; there was no danger of running off or overturning!

His hand went down to change gears; the beat of the engine suddenly altered to a deep growl. They had turned out of the bush and were sliding down a sandy track. Through a cutting between great fine-grained silver sand dunes they slithered, the engine taking on an even deeper note. Abruptly they were out in the open, and Nicola was not the only one to gasp. The ocean was rushing at them, breaker upon breaker, iridescent blue-green monsters, foam-capped as they swirled to crash upon the hard-packed sand below high water mark. Only the silver sheen of fine white powder surrounding the edge of the guarding dunes remained beyond their reach.

The driver glanced at her across the intervening space, and smiled. This was his beach. He loved it. And it was so obvious he would like anyone who felt the same way. Expertly turning the heavy transport, he sent it leaping forward along the edge of the ocean. As it flew along even the chatting passengers in the back were silent. Wide, empty, the beach stretched before them: the rushing, tumultuous turquoise blue on one side: white dunes of sand towering above the flying vehicle on the other. Silhouetted along these heights the ubiquitous she-oaks stretched forth their wind-tossed, stunted branches.

A wonderful vista, breathtaking in its scope, it was no wonder that for the time being talking was forsaken in favour of just experiencing. It was their driver who interrupted Nicola's fascinated viewing as he reached down to change gears for the second time.

'Nearly there, my girl,' he said. 'I'll let you out right opposite a track winding up from the beach to the headland.' He glanced thoughtfully at her cases and a cardboard carton, telling her regretfully, 'I'll take those to the foot of the cliff, but I can't leave my passengers and go wandering off.' He jerked his head backwards.

'No, I realise that, thank you, Mr Torrens. You've been most helpful, and I'll manage very well. I'm used to fending for myself. I intend only to stay a couple of days, you know, just to look round and check things. There are some people here almost always, aren't there?'

'Yes,' she had answer. 'There's old Pete who keeps an eye on things generally, if you need to get a message down to us. Then, of course, there's this new outfit, although they're further along, more towards the cattle country. The boss of that seems a decent bloke, and he uses our barge ...' He stopped speaking, braking to a standstill below one of the highest dunes of the whole coastline. 'Here we are,' he was continuing, opening his door and beginning to haul her luggage down. 'I'll carry these to the track,' he told her, pointing to the big suitcase and the carton of groceries. 'They're much too heavy for a slip of a girl like you to lug.'

Her seldom used warm smile gave thanks, and,

grasping her overnight case, she trailed after him. A few paces and she was off the hard wet sand and trudging through the silver-fine powder that gave to this place its look of shining brilliance. It pulled at her sandals and the case in her hand began to weigh more than she had thought it ever could. Impedimenta set down at the tiny path beginning to wend its way upwards along the side of the cliff face, Mr Torrens was already making his way back.

'My schedule depends on the tide, Miss Grant,' he told her somewhat apologetically. 'If I'm late I'm caught, because the beach is covered with water and I can't risk that. So I'm afraid I'll have to leave you to manage. It's not too far, though.'

'Of course you must go, and thanks for what you've already done. . . .' Nicola found, however, that she was speaking to a form already hurrying away, a hand waving casually over a shoulder. She stood there, the vastness of empty space around her, and watched the Land Rover diminish into the distance, and for a brief moment a feeling of abandonment possessed her.

Her whole worldly possessions grouped about her, she remained at the bottom of the high dune, looking, if the truth were told, more than a trifle disconsolate. Then with a shrug of acceptance she bent and took up in both arms the container of groceries and her small overnight case. Kicking off her sandals, she left them lying in the sand and stepped on to the upward winding trail. It was a steep climb, though a short one, and she came out on to a flat, coarsely grassed headland. A hundred yards or so opposite her was the house.

It appeared a whole lot smaller than her childhood memories of it, but as she plodded through the yielding grass with its underlying carpet of sand, it took on the familiarity of knowledge. Her father must have been an orderly sort of person, judging by this part of the property. There was not a piece of litter on the—she supposed it could be called lawn of a sort, and although the paint was faded, the entire place appeared clean and well kept. It was the same inside, she found.

Stepping awkwardly over the small raised cement step with her burden in her arms, she looked around for somewhere to deposit it. There was a table at the end of what was apparently the one big room of the living quarters. She noticed, as she dropped the heavy box containing the wherewithal to survive for the next few days upon it, that it was made of old-fashioned wood and scrubbed to whiteness. An assessing glance about her and she decided that at least the place was liveable in for the short time she would be here. It was bare, austere even, but it was clean. A dresser, also old-fashioned like the table, occupied one side of a wall, and a sink stood beside it near a window. Two canvas chairs turned towards the small shaded verandah completed the furnishings. She walked slowly to the door of the main bedroom and stood in its opening.

A double bed was pushed against the far wall, its mattress rolled up with a look of long disuse, and under the window a stretcher bed stood; austere, with its hospital neatness of tightly pulled blankets and sheets. The room was dark, stuffy. She moved past the chest of drawers and reached for the cord of the roller-blind, giving it a quick tug. It swung up with a clatter and she pushed urgently at the window sash. Flinging the last of these wide, she stood motionless.

The scene that struck at her could have been the setting for songs, for poetry ... not ballads or sonnets, but the wildness of a full soaring grand operatic. The harsh branches of the she-oaks sketched their shadows starkly against the vividness of cerulean skies. Tumbling water, lapis lazuli, milky jade, white-capped, crashed upon firm unyielding sand, and the gleam of silver that edged the beginning of the shallow cliffs followed the vast coastline as it unfolded mile after uncounted mile. Suddenly, unexpectedly, Nicola wanted this place; it was hers, she would keep it. Childish memories came echoing through the mists of time, and childish words, pushed into the dark recesses of a mind not wanting to remember until this moment, reverberated.

'Why are we leaving, Mummy? I love it here, I don't want to go. When we will be coming back? When...?'

And the answer was there also in her memories, forgotten long ago until she gazed out at this scene before her; at this beach upon which a child had played.

'Tomorrow, darling. We'll come back tomorrow.'

But that tomorrow had never come. Today she had returned, and in a little while she would be twenty. Far away, and so lonely, this land of tomorrow that she was now looking at was something that had provided comfort, until gradually, as the seasons followed one another in the march of the years, it had been lost among them. Her sudden intention hardened. This place was hers, she would keep it.

Retracing her steps, she made her way back down the track and retrieved the rest of her possessions. About three o'clock, the noonday heat declining somewhat—a swim was in order, she decided. She had earned one too, she thought. She had thoroughly explored, and worked, and found that though a trifle primitive all the facilities were adequate.

Tea made on the old-fashioned Primus turned out just as she liked it, steaming and fragrant. Fresh bread and butter from her cardboard container provided the type of sandwiches produced only by specialists in their field. Taking up her simple lunch, she pulled one of the canvas chairs into the shade on the verandah, and there ate slowly, her gaze upon the tumbling, crashing, ever-moving water.

Finally she rose, and inside, washed the used dishes, stacked them away. Changing into a bikini (not one of the latest ones, she admitted, without any desire to acquire such a possession) applying sun-tan oil generously, she caught up her towelling wrap and made her way down the winding path to the beach.

So she wasn't the only human in the world after all, she noticed, as she crossed the few paces to stand at the water's edge. Looking south towards civilisation, a solitary fisherman was seen standing thigh-deep in the creaming surf making a cast from a rod which seemed at least twice as big as a rod should be. Her glance travelled in the other direction towards the famous Coloured Sands. Away in the far distance, haze-obscured, were some black dots in the edge of the water. Trying to focus, an upflung hand shading her eyes from the glare, Nicola knew they were too far away for her to perceive if they were swimmers or fishermen.

Tyre tracks from the four-wheeled drives criss-crossed the surface where she was standing. Idly she wondered if Mr Torren's marks from this morning's trip would be among them, or if they had already been washed away, then high-stepping through the waves to waist level, she swam back and forth parallel to the beach. This was the first time in her life she had swum absolutely alone, and almost the only time she could remember not swimming in a surf-club patrolled area.

It was a delight to be in the water, warm and crystal-clear, the waves coming one on top of another. But dumped under by a larger than average wave for the second time in as many minutes, she decided that the tide was on the turn, and enough was enough, and allowed the swell to carry her into shore.

Making a leisurely way to her towel, that lay, an object of brightness on the stretch of empty sand, she picked it up, patting at the surplus moisture upon her body. And, leisurely again, she stooped to gather a shell, perfect in its purity, that she had nearly trodden upon, and stepped directly into the path of a Land

Rover careering swiftly along the beach. If she hadn't been daydreaming she would have heard it.

A vision of an exasperated scowl on deeply tanned features, the flash of white teeth in another face just as bronzed, as the second figure in the passenger seat turned to wave, caught at her vision in the brief moment before the vehicle had passed. It left her with the impression of a driver showing plainly what he thought of suicidal fools, as he swung the wheel sharply to avoid her.

Standing there gazing after the Rover as it careered in the direction of the black dots in the distance she had noticed earlier, Nicola realised how stupid she had been. Subconsciously she had heard the noise of the engine, but the fact hadn't registered, the luminous shell having caught her eye at the very moment the car had been passing. With a whole wide empty beach, no driver would expect a girl to walk deliberately in front of his vehicle; certainly that driver had not thought it. She remembered ruefully again the annoyed look he had flung in her direction. Well, there it was. With a final shrug she ran across the sand and marched quickly up the incline, over the lawn and into her house.

CHAPTER TWO

DRAGGING one of the deck chairs across to the table, Nicola arranged the old-fashioned hurricane light to focus more clearly over her shoulder. The book, however, lay in her lap unheeded. To a town-orientated girl, there was a feeling of eeriness knowing herself alone in the almost immeasurable silence about her; for silence was there. Even the ocean had quietened down to a mere murmur.

Behind half-closed lids, her head back against the chair-rest, she thought of her father's death, of the long-ago past that seemed to be in the room with her. Older now, she realised that it hadn't been indifference to her on her father's part, or even lack of love. It had been the overriding necessity to watch and guard a woman he loved beyond anything else, a woman who had been so ill for a long time.

'Why am I called Nicola, Mummy?' the small girl had asked once. 'It's a funny name for a girl!'

'Because you're all the family we'll have, darling,' she had been answered sadly, 'and I wanted it to be like Daddy's name. Don't you think it's lovely to be called that?'

'Yes ... I expect so.' She had answered obediently, but she had thought it would have been twice as lovely to have a glamorous name such as Marilyn, or Gloria, like one little girl she knew.

However, here she was now, and a new life in Brisbane was opening ahead of her in a few days' time. Determinedly she pushed away the past and concentrated on the printed page. Words were beginning to take shape and meaning, when there came a knock on the front door.

Startled and—yes, frightened a little, she rose and stood upright. The knock came again. She moved towards the door, asking:

'Who is it?'

'It's Andrew Huntly, Miss Grant. Could I see you for a minute?' The words came slightly muffled by the thick plank door.

She had no idea who Andrew Huntly might be, but he knew her name and the voice sounded reassuring, so she slid back the bolt and pulled open the door.

He was standing beneath the overhang, and it was dark out there, only the stars giving illumination to the vastness of space enclosing them. Even the white-topped waves were invisible. Her uninvited visitor moved inside, into the uncertain brightness the hurricane lamp was giving forth. He remained there, glancing about him.

He was the driver of the Land Rover of this afternoon, she saw at once: the one who had looked his exasperation at the foolishness of someone who, with forty miles of wide open, empty beach around, had almost stepped under the wheels of the solitary vehicle upon it.

Her impression of brownness, of tanned features, had been right, she decided, waiting for him to speak. In the faint half-light playing upon him, the face could have been carved from polished bronze. His hair had a lightness that contrasted with that so brown skin, and was straight, heavy, forming a cap of smoothness over the arrogantly held head. Indistinguishable under straight brows drawn almost together now in a frown of impatience, the colour of his eyes remained hidden.

He turned from his inspection of the room and said matter-of-factly, curtly, the tone of a man used to saying what he wanted done, and expecting to have his orders obeyed:

'I've come to take you up to the resort, Miss Grant. You can't stay here alone. I only learned of your arrival while we were having dinner. Torrens told Sarah when he pulled in with a load of supplies.' His piece spoken, he waited.

Nicola didn't know how to answer this direction, taken aback by his dictatorial 'I've come to take you' not a 'Will you come?' request.

'Thank you,' she then got out, 'but I'm all right here. I'm only remaining for a couple of days. Besides, I simply don't want to come up to any resort, wherever it is.'

A few yards apart, they stood gazing at each other—a stand-off. Then, apparently not accustomed to someone outwaiting him, the man remarked with expectation of acquiescence implicit in each inflection, 'This is no place for a girl alone. It's a law-abiding region, I'm aware, but it's also starting to get popular with dune-buggy riders. Until we get a little law domiciled here, they're beginning to burn along the beach, out for a night's sport. So you're not staying here by yourself. I have a young sister, and I would expect anyone to do the same for her—if she was ever in the same situation.'

By the inflection in his tone, Nicola gathered that he would never dream of allowing a sister of his to be in such a situation.

She merely replied again, 'It's very kind of you, Mr Huntly, but I would prefer to stay here.' There was dismissal in her words.

'No doubt you might! I'll tell you something, however,' his tone of voice had changed, not as she would have expected, to hardness at opposition, but to a soft drawl. 'You're not going to stay here. Get whatever you need for the night and we'll go.'

As she still made no effort to comply, his voice became even softer ... silken. 'I'm turning out this light in five seconds, and you're coming with me—one way or another. The sand might make walking with a burden a little difficult, but I imagine I can manage it.'

Again they looked at one another, and Nicola knew he meant precisely what he said. She could be determined too. But though wanting badly to defy his ultimatum, she knew she would be going. It would be better to go in a dignified manner.

She walked towards the bedroom door. The man picked up the lamp by its looped handle and followed. He raised it high, enabling her to see as she took the nightdress and dressing-gown which were folded across the bottom of the made-up stretcher bed and crammed them into her overnight case.

As she finished packing, she looked at him again with the intention of talking it over sensibly. 'Mr Huntly...?'

'Yes.' There was no expression at all in the word; just one flat syllable.

She looked directly at him: at the eyes half-hooded, the stance indolent as he leant against the door-frame, and suddenly she couldn't make herself go on. Those eyes—what colour were they? And was it only the uncertain light that made her think of a word like sinister?

'Nothing.... It doesn't matter. I have everything I want.' And she had, even if her words sounded a little breathless.

Reaching out then, he shut the windows with a bang and stood aside. Waiting until she reached the open front door, he flicked the small lever of the lamp, raised the glass and blew. Abruptly they were in utter darkness. Without having heard any sound of movement at all, Nicola felt fingers grip her upper arm lightly, then the door was firmly closed as she was piloted through. Observing no attempt made to lock it, she reflected acidly that he obviously didn't believe it would be burgled and all her belongings stolen. Yet he couldn't allow her to stay there!

In her heeled sandals, she made heavy work of walking through the yielding sand to the edge of the headland. The fingers loosened their clasp of her arm and slid downwards to take hold of her hand. His voice, above her head, told her, 'Here, put your hand on my other shoulder, and take off those unsuitable shoes.'

Because in this also he was right, she did as she was bid. Standing on one foot and then on the other, hanging on to his shoulder, she eased off the offending footgear and swung them both from one hand. He returned his grasp to her elbow and she walked beside him effortlessly in bare feet.

Her vision becoming accustomed to the darkness, she could distinguish the waves now and the faint outline of their white-capped tops as they slid calmly in to the beach, while the breeze-caressed branches silhouetted against the sky rattled as they passed beneath. Her companion asked suddenly from out of the night:

'Torrens told us you were Grant's daughter. Have you just come along to see the property?'

'Yes.' The one word answered him.

A short silence, then, 'What else is your name beside Grant? What do they call you?'

'Nicola.'

It sounded so bald, and—yes, rude. After all, he was older than she was, and was only doing what he thought was right. She said again, 'Nicola, after my ... my father.' Having so seldom had reason to speak that word, she found it hard to utter now. 'His name was Nicholas, and as I was an only child, my mother called me the nearest thing to his name.'

'Uhuh.' It could not be called anything so raucous as a snort—still, the sound defied analysis.

Reaching the Rover, he put her into the offside seat, and once again, as she had this morning, she was flying over the hard-packed sand. This time, however, it seemed so very different, closed in by the darkness of night, instead of surrounded by blazing sunshine. Swiftly as they went, it seemed only a short time before he spoke again.

'Here we are!'

Nicola put out a hand to grab hold of a projection as the car tilted suddenly and she saw that they were riding upon a corduroy ramp which went slantwise along the cliff-side. It appeared as solid as a cement parking ramp, and an ideal vehicle access for the locality it served. Emerging off this contraption between two towering dunes of sand, she was abruptly transplanted to a different world from the empty, silent beach, the infinity of space, they had just left down by the ocean.

This was the more familiar world of luxurious motels ... sparkling, expensive. Through either plate glass, or space, unable to be distinguished from this distance, they could look right into a large dining-room and lounge. Bright lights, the movement of people, the echo of laughter and music, came wafting across to them as they sat quiet for a moment after the sound of the engine died away. Nicola's companion helped her down and they stood, his hand still clasping hers while looking across at this picture framed in light.

'Seeing this as a newcomer, a stranger, would you say it looks as if it might be a successful venture?' he asked.

She turned to glance up at him, in truth, not knowing what to reply, then answered the only thing she could. 'How can you ask? In this setting? With that complex? And that wonderful beach on its very doorstep ... that lovely stretch of nature's bounty ... what else could it be but a success?'

He laughed suddenly, amusement for the first time tonight apparent in the very timbre of his voice as he remarked, 'I'd forgotten how young you were. Young, and of course, romantic. I'm afraid, though, that this place was not established for romantics. It's for fishing, and, for those who want it, riding among cattle. This stretch of ocean is one of the few unspoilt fishing localities around the capital, and all of that'—he threw out a hand in a throw-away gesture towards the long curving stretch of silver sand hidden now in the darkness'—is but an added attraction. Therefore I hope to see a lot of fishermen. The beauty of it, also, is that fish bite better in the freezing cold of a winter's night than in the summer, so I expect to have the place a going concern in all seasons.'

Nicola had barely taken in his discourse about fishing and horse-riding in her indignation at his use of the word romantic in connection with her. It was the last description she would have applied to herself, and that fact came out in her ejaculation.

'Romantic? I'm not romantic—not one little bit! I've had no time to indulge in such ethereal nonsense.

I've been too busy making a life for myself.' She repeated again flatly, 'I'm not a romantic!'

His hand shifted and both came upon her shoulders, turning her towards him. He gazed down at her, and once more she caught the flash of whiteness in the near dark: this time in a smile, before he spoke.

'Come off it, Nicola—of course you're romantic! Why, your description of the beach had romance in the very sound. What fisherman would call it "lovely"? They would come down and look at the ocean, taking no notice of the beach at all, wet a finger, hold it to the wind, cast an eye over the water, and say, either: "Beaut! The fish should be right today", or, "The raking breeze is in the south-east, no decent fishing today". But they'd still be off with their rods ... and their creels. Hope springs eternal with fishermen, you know!' His tone changed abruptly, the amusement leaving it. 'Come along,' he added. 'We'll get you settled in.'

On a path indistinctly seen in the light streaming from the enormous building before them, Nicola trod first in one sandal, then into the other. Her footsteps now rang out as she walked along it. In a transition that seemed almost too abrupt, they were in a room full of people. Andrew Huntly led her to a tall, erect middle-aged woman, hair blue-rinsed and perfectly coiffured—a proper martinet she looked, thought the unwanting-to-be-here, uninvited guest.

'I've brought you Miss Nicola Grant, Sarah,' her companion was saying. 'We can put her up in one of the empty staff units for the night, can't we?'

Nicola glanced at this somewhat awe-inspiring woman, feeling butterflies start fluttering in the region of her diaphragm, wondering about her reception. She found herself engulfed in a warm smile and a hand reached out in welcome.

'Of course we can, Drew. How are you, my dear? You'll be much better off here with us, you know, than up in that isolated place on your own. Come along and meet the rest, then I'll take you to your room. If you came with Mr Torrens this morning, you'll have had a long day.' She turned to the man beside her. 'All right, Peter—it appears that she's Nicola Grant. Peter Sinclair, my dear. He's Drew's manager here, and much as it goes against the grain to say such a thing about someone as irresponsible as he is, I have to admit I think he'll make a very good one.'

'Thank you, Sarah, even if it is a back-handed compliment. But you're quite right, you know. Because Drew being Drew, I wouldn't be here if such wasn't the case.' This man had the flashing smile she had noticed this afternoon and he turned the full force of it upon her, saying,

'Nicola! Now there's a name to give one pause. May I call you by it? I don't know how long you'll be here, so I have to make hay while the sun shines.'

She nodded, thinking how like other such men he was: the ones she had known in the big engineering firm in which she had worked—competent, confident, so sure of themselves and the fact that the world was their oyster. She knew how to deal with such advances, which even though innocuous, were made only to amuse their own egos. So she gave to him her reserved, cool smile, turning as her abductor's voice cut in:

'This is Elspeth Percival, Nicola, only here for a couple of days, worse luck.'

Glancing up to say 'How do you do', Nicola almost gasped. This woman was beautiful—tall, with a figure to make most eyes turn, raven black hair drawn back in an unfashionable straight swathe to lie in a sculptured roll upon her neck. Eyebrows to match that so dark hair were like wings in flight above the largest hazel eyes Nicola had ever seen. Full lips outlined with —this time, very fashionable—pale lipstick. In spite of all this beauty, however, to the younger girl just arrived in this brightly-lighted room, she showed none of its warmth. Nicola was glad when Sarah cut in on their stilted exchanges.

'Come along, my dear. An early night is indicated for us all tonight.'

She came along, taking the case Drew Huntly handed to her, and followed the older woman through a big echoing kitchen to the back exit. She turned over the idea of Drew for Andrew Huntly. She knew she didn't like him; she would never like him, because of his attitude tonight. He was worse than Peter's sort in thinking he owned the earth; but Drew sounded so much more likeable than the more formal Andrew.

'We've put you in one of the staff rooms for tonight, Nicola,' Sarah's voice broke in upon these meditations.

'We're opening in a few days' time. Everything is still at sixes and sevens as yet, but with Drew at the helm, things will straighten themselves out.'

'Does this belong to him, Sarah? In these modern times it's usually companies who control these kind of complexes.' Nicola was on firm ground here, having worked her way up in a big company which had a great deal to do with building these conglomerations.

'Well, it's a kind of syndicate, I expect you could say. I have some money in it. A lot of his sister's is too; also family finance. The land itself belongs to a cattle property they own. Everything is being diversified these days, so it was decided to open this complex and co-opt it with the cattle property.'

'Mr Huntly would be the last person I could see running a holiday resort. Diplomacy would be classed a necessity for such a venture, I would imagine, and my impression of him. . . .' Nicola spread outflung hands before continuing her progress. She spoke in a tone that was anything but unbiased, because she felt entitled to utter some kind of disparagement. She felt it owing for the behaviour to which she had been subjected just a little while ago.

Sarah only laughed softly, however, as she turned in under the overhang of a unit and groped for the door handle, saying over her shoulder:

'You couldn't be more right, Nicola, only Drew won't be running it. That's Peter's job. Peter has just returned from Spain where he's been furthering his trade—and don't let his easy-going attitude fool you.

He's an expert at his work, and a different person when he's on the job.' Sarah flicked a switch through the open door, then stood back.

Walking into the room, Nicola stood gazing about her. It was for two, she noticed, as she took in the twin beds on either side of the walls. Above head height, the windows operated with a lever which needed only one flick to have them wide open as they were now, or closed if needed in bad weather. Angled, they would catch a sea breeze the whole twenty-four hours. The furniture was in light silver wood—and if this was staff accommodation, she reflected, what would the guests' rooms be like?

Making short work of undressing, she was soon in bed, the long day whirling chaotically about her. The loveliness and infinity of space that was the beach was her most vivid impression, but two faces were also there. One, closed up, unapproachable, light brown head, brown tanned face, eyes ... what colour were they? she wondered. But she didn't like him! Now Peter—that was another matter. He would be easy to get on with, easy to like, very.... She was asleep.

CHAPTER THREE

Hot fingers of light stretching from a sun just beginning its climb to the heavens played hide and seek among the buildings, then on to and through the big row of glass windows. Nicola stretched, put up a hand to shade half-open eyes from a dazzling brightness that suddenly bombarded them. Abruptly, taking in her surroundings, she was awake, and yesterday's happenings brought vividly to mind by the sight of the strange room. She glanced at her watch.

Good heavens! A quarter to eight. She swung her feet out of bed and groping for slippers or scuffs, discovered only the heeled sandals that brought back the memory of a teak-hard, wide shoulder, on which she had leaned.

Slipping her feet into them, she reached for her dressing gown. Opening the door a trifle nervously, she peered outside. There was no one about—oh yes, there was! Further away on a small rise was a unit isolated from its fellows by a trellis upon which a shining green-leafed vine was beginning to creep. Towards one side of it were three horses.

Nicola noticed that they were work horses, not

thoroughbreds or show hacks, and that on two of them sat youths in the universal costume of tight jeans and faded coloured shirts.

A leg hooked high over the pommel, one of the riders was taking in his surroundings with an inquisitive eye, no attention at all being given to the cigarette he was rolling between a tiny piece of fragile white paper with the expertise of long practice.

She must have made a movement, because unexpectedly, glancing across the distance separating them, he winked. Caught somehow off guard, Nicola swung round, and made her way swiftly along the small paved walkaway to the shower block. She had to smile, though. The cheek of him! It had been such a merry wink, as if for him there could not possibly be someone who was not his friend.

Back in her room, dressed, and her night attire packed, she stood gazing indecisively at the unmade bed, deciding finally to leave it as it was until she had seen Sarah. She would probably remain here for the night, but she would be leaving the beach tomorrow on her way to Brisbane.

Still seeing no one around this part of the resort, Nicola made her way along one of the little cement paths to the door she thought she had emerged from last night. Standing before one of the big electric ranges along the far wall, a woman turned as she entered, large, comfortable, with a welcome on her pleasant face as she said, 'Here you are, my dear. Mr Huntly said to let you be until you woke by yourself. Now, what would you like for breakfast?'

'Oh, fruit juice, if I may, and a cup of tea and toast, please.'

'You young ones! No appreciation for proper meals at all,' came spiralling across to her.

'Oh, here you are, Nicola.' Sarah's greeting saved her from answering. She had entered from the dining-room. 'I hope you had a good sleep, and have you told Mrs Hill what you would like for breakfast?' At Nicola's nod, she turned, saying, 'Come along, then.'

The young girl followed her hostess and sat at the table indicated. Through the vast expanse of glass en-circling them she saw on the skyline the familiar she-oaks lifting their twisted branches to meet the ocean breeze. She gazed out also at gardens and lawns, smooth bright emerald lawns, alien to this environ-ment, reaching right away towards the dunes that guarded the coastline.

Mrs Hill came in with the food—Sarah's, Nicola noticed, the same as her own.

'Drew and Peter will be in directly, Mrs Hill. Is their meal ready?' asked Sarah.

'Yes, it is, and not what you're having, either!' Satis-faction flowed through the housekeeper's words as she sailed back to the kitchen.

Nicola was wondering how to bring up the subject of her room when a stir at the doorway announced the men Sarah had just mentioned. She raised the glass of orange juice to her lips, giving to it all her attention.

'Good morning, Nicola. Any comment on our estab-lishment I'll accept for processing.' Peter grinned across at her as he pulled out his chair. Before she could formulate a reply, the man on her other side put in his penny's worth.

'Good morning, Nicola.'

A greeting only, with no additional comment. He was giving his attention to the food Mrs Hill was placing before him, and Nicola noticed that it wasn't just tea and toast that he and Peter had for breakfast. Surreptitiously she looked him over. Yes, he was tanned; tanned a deep dark bronze; his hair light against it. Unexpectedly, his glance came up, and his eyes, grey, rain-washed, reserved, inspected her. Meeting that gaze, she felt a surge of pink colour her features. Of course, he would look up and catch her examining him! she thought wrathfully.

As suddenly as they had been raised, the eyes were lowered, and he was busy plying a knife and fork among the food on his plate. Peter was doing likewise. His eyes, blue, gay, uncomplicated, scanned the room. He asked with a mouth half full:

'Where's the charming doctor this morning? Isn't breakfast a habit she indulges in?'

After waiting out a moment's silence, it was Sarah who replied, dryness in her normally even tone.

'She informed me last night that she'd give breakfast a miss to get some much-needed rest, Drew having just said he'd be leaving at daybreak for the homestead to catch his uncle.'

'She probably does need rest, Sarah,' Drew broke in softly. 'She works very hard, and puts in long hours too, you know.'

Nicola sat silent throughout these cross-currents. She wondered who the doctor was.

'Yes, I expect she does. I expect, though, that Elspeth is only here to inspect this establishment. You've been spending so much of your time here lately that she wants to see it for herself.' There it was again, that funny tone in Sarah's voice.

But her words had astounded Nicola. That lovely woman whom she had met last night . . . a doctor? Who would have believed it? To be as perfect as the impression she presented would need a lot of time and work put into accomplishing such an effect. She said, not meaning the words to come out as loudly as they did:

'I would never have imagined her a doctor. I would have thought she'd never had to lift a finger on such a sordid thing as work.'

'Oh, yes, she's a doctor all right, and if reports speak truly, a very good one,' Sarah answered her amazed words.

The rest of the breakfast conversation consisted of subjects like underground tanks, stresses and pressures. However, when Sarah rose, and Nicola with her, Drew turned to the older woman. 'Most of the staff will be coming across on the barge this afternoon. Tell Mrs Hill, will you? They can make a start of getting this,' he threw out a hand at the bare tables, 'in shape tomorrow. The first of our guests arrive on Friday evening.'

Sarah asked, 'Will the place be full, Drew?'

It was Peter who answered. 'We think so. We've filled it at a reduced rate for the service clubs. They seemed pleased to accept the offer, and it's their reports we're hoping will advertise it.'

'Yes, well. . . .' Sarah made to walk off and Nicola pushed in her chair, preparing to follow, but a voice stopped her. 'Nicola, spare me a moment, please, I'd like a word with you.'

She remained there uncertainly as Sarah departed. Peter continued eating as his boss rose and taking Nicola's arm, piloted her outside. Walking beside him, she took the path he indicated towards the gaily painted table with its matching chairs which stood among others on the terrace that ran the whole length of the resort. The man remained silent for a while after they were seated, gazing out over the grounds.

He began speaking slowly as if searching for words. 'I was talking to Torrens about some stuff I wanted ferrying across the barge, and he asked me if I'd seen you. He told me you're not going back up north.' Nicola twisted restlessly, angry at her affairs being discussed all over the place. Her companion must have taken note of this and guessed its reason. 'Anyone's affairs are everybody's business in small country towns, you know,' he answered her indignation. 'He told me you were going south to work, that you'd brought all your belongings down here to this part of the state. Would this be so?'

'Yes.' The reply was a single word, and she wondered where on earth this conversation was leading, and too, what business was it of his. She was further annoyed at his next words.

'What exactly was your job up north, Nicola?'

Again, she didn't want to answer him, a strange reluctance overtaking her, then she shrugged and told him, 'I was private secretary to the managing director of a large construction firm.'

'I expect you had to do some receptionist work in the course of your duties?'

'Among other things, if important people wanted to see my boss, yes, I did.' She was still only giving strictly information replies.

'I've a proposition to make, then. Could you see yourself joining us as a receptionist?' He lifted a hand to restrain her as she made to speak. 'Hear me out,' he added, his gaze still fastened in the direction of the beach. 'There would be advantages as well as disadvantages, you know. You would be classed with Peter, because I need someone I can trust behind the desk—not just an ordinary typist. Emergencies could arise in which you would have to use your discretion, and, most important of all,' her companion was continuing, 'you would have to have expertise enough to smooth over any little awkwardness that might arise when Peter is not available ... he must have time off for himself.

'You would also,' he turned to her fully now, 'have your own suite, all the swimming you wanted, and there'll be social activities as we get going. I guess you wouldn't have the excitement and the rush and bustle of the city, and that fact could be important to a young girl. Well, would you be interested?' The last sentence came curtly.

She brought her gaze round to his face, and, as she had so unexpectedly at breakfast, looked into the deep slate-grey eyes, that were so startling against the intense bronze of the surrounding skin.

She backed sharply away from the hitherto unknown emotion this encounter produced, and in her turn glanced away and over the grounds. The terse refusal she had meant to utter remained unspoken. She didn't want to remain here, she didn't like Andrew Huntly, but somehow she didn't want to refuse this job, either. Without looking at him the words came out.

'All right, Mr Huntly, I'll accept. Only for a trial period, though.'

'Fair enough, Nicola. We'll both be on trial—you, to see if you like it, I, to see if you're satisfactory. But I'm afraid I'm not Mr Huntly to you. We expect to be a happy family here, and if you can manage Peter as Peter, I'm afraid you'll have to manage Drew as well. Now,' he stood up, 'I'll get Jim to run you up in the Rover to collect your belongings. You can then settle in to your own accommodation. The room you occupied last night will be needed by staff coming up this evening.'

As they moved towards the complex, suddenly, it was fun to be here, in this beautiful setting as unlike a workaday job as could be imagined. 'I expect you'd better get together with Peter,' her ... employer, she recognised now, spoke crisply, 'and find your way around among our brochures, and our units. I would like you to be able to answer most questions fired at you when the first intake arrives here on Friday evening. As you'll be gone all day tomorrow you'll need to cram as much as you can in today.'

'Where will I be all day tomorrow?' she echoed.

'You'll be in Brisbane. I still have a hundred things to see to, besides having to take Elspeth back. I have also to make arrangements for Candace, who arrives home next week. The reason you're coming too is to get uniforms. Elspeth has worked out a colour combination, and even Sarah,' here his tone went as dry as Sarah's had been this morning at the breakfast table, 'gives it her complete approval. I'll drop you in at the salon which, I hope, will have them finished by the time we're ready to come home.'

Will it, though? thought Nicola. Talk about high-handedness! She asked curtly, 'What kind of uniforms?'

She looked up and caught his eyes, unexpectedly they were dancing; sparkling teasingly, although his mouth remained grave.

He remarked in that deceptively soft voice of his, 'Wouldn't you care to wear a uniform, Nicola! I assure you we won't dress you up like a slave girl—or is it the colour scheme you object to?'

She remained silent under those glinting eyes, thinking she was no match for this man, and quite content to be handed over to Peter when they arrived inside.

If she had had any thought of being offered a sine-cure, she was soon disillusioned on that score. For the whole of that day Peter kept her hard at it. She vowed too, as he explained and showed, that no one would have cause to question her efficiency. So it was a very tired girl who, after a quick shower and the donning of a simple cotton frock, made her way to dinner that night.

In the kitchen, she was introduced by Mrs Hill to the four girls already there, busy in both the staff dining room and the vast tourist area from which it opened off. Moving into this, she found it empty, but through the archway into the bar the others were milling about.

Drew must have been on the look-out, for he came towards her, guiding her across to them. The room and people around her receded into another dimension; the only thing in her conscious thoughts were those fingers about her arm, tensile, firm, sending an alto-gether strange sensation through her whole nervous system. Then she did notice something; those beauti-ful eyes of Elspeth's were upon her, raking over her entire body. And Nicola, having previously felt she looked suitable for an informal dinner, felt suddenly dressed in rags.

Shoving a tall bar stool towards her, Peter grinned, and Sarah smiled kindly. Drew went behind the counter and passed across a small crystal glass filled with an amber liquid. Nicola took the sherry and sipped, and gradually found that she wasn't dressed in rags after all.

Peter remarked in his casual way, 'You picked a winner in young Nicola here, Drew. I wouldn't go so far as to say she knows as much about this place as I do, but she isn't far behind. Instead of my slave-driving her, it's she who has been doing the slave-driving. She should fit in very nicely behind that front reception desk.'

Elspeth's voice, cold and showing almost a spurt of anger, cut through the small silence into which Peter's words had fallen. 'What do you mean, Peter? Miss Grant isn't going to work here, is she?' And, as he nodded, she went on, 'I thought she'd just come down to check on her little shack. I didn't realise she was also searching for a job!'

In the world of big business which was Nicola's workaday environment, she had often met up with the equivalent of other Elspeths. She was quite able to reply in kind.

'I came down to look over my little shack, certainly; and I wasn't particularly looking for a job, but the terms of this one being so generous, I couldn't resist it.' She raised the small glass to her lips in a salute to them all, and drank. Before she could reach over and set it on the bar, it was taken from her hand, and Drew's voice, drawn through a silken mesh, said, 'Dinner, I think!'

This meal was a very different affair from breakfast, or for that matter, lunch, which, with Sarah, Nicola had gone into the kitchen to collect. Tonight they were seated in state at a table which was set with damask, silver and glass.

'A rehearsal,' Sarah remarked a trifle caustically, 'for Friday night.'

Nicola ate the meal, spoke when spoken to, then asked to be excused from coffee in the lounge. She was turning from the table by herself towards the back entrance, when, unexpectedly, a man's figure was walking beside her.

'Have you shifted, Nicola?' it asked. 'Are your quarters satisfactory? I'd like to check them myself and be satisfied too.'

She really didn't want him checking her quarters. But what she wanted didn't cut much ice, apparently. He came inside with her, cast an assessing glance over the whole unit—guest accommodation, Nicola had realised when being shifted into it, knowing full well she would have been quite satisfied with staff quarters.

He gazed across at her now, standing rigidly just inside the doorway, back against the partition, and an eyebrow went up. 'You're quite safe, Nicola,' he told her softly. 'I'm not going to rape you ... not tonight, anyway. Relax a little.'

She went even straighter. Rape indeed! What a thing to say. But he was walking past her through the doorway, pausing there only to say, 'I'm afraid it's a six o'clock call in the morning for you; but as you know, the saying is, time and tide wait for no man, and it's the tide that won't wait for us. Goodnight, sleep well.' He was gone.

CHAPTER FOUR

SOMEONE was calling. Nicola wished they would go away, but the noise continued. Rising up through layers of deep sleep, she heard a voice say, 'A quarter to six, Miss Grant, there's a cup of tea ready, but Mr Huntly doesn't want to be late.'

'Okay, Jim—thanks! I'm coming.'

Showering in double-quick time, she slipped into clothes she had prepared the night before, applied a light touch of lipstick, then caught up a cardigan and her handbag. Fifteen minutes from the time Jim had called her, she was in the kitchen doorway.

They were all in the bright room, including Elspeth. Like last night, Nicola received a kind smile from Sarah, a nod from Drew, no acknowledgement at all from Elspeth, and a cup of hot tea with a plate of buttery toast from Mrs Hill. Carrying it to one of the benches, she sipped the liquid, thinking absently that small things added their quota of contentment to life —things like the day's first cup of tea, or a bright kitchen with shining utensils.

Drew finished his, picked up a sweater lying on the bench beside him and held it while Elspeth slid her arms in, then he was beside Nicola, asking:

'Did you bring a jumper, Nicola? Summer it may be, but it will be cool driving along that open beach in the Land Rover.' He followed the direction of her glance, and then it was her turn to have a cardigan held for her to don. She felt his fingers upon her neck as he lifted the hair to drop it outside the covering, then the presence at her back was no longer there. She followed the exodus outside.

Her employer helped Elspeth up the high steps into the front seat, then moved round to the back to ensconce Sarah before turning to Nicola. For the first time this morning he looked directly at her, and his voice from above asked softly:

'Did you sleep well on your first night of belonging to us, Nicola? No untoward visitors disturbed your virgin slumber, I hope?' Not waiting, or for that matter seeming to expect a reply, he put out a hand to help her into the waiting transport.

Safely seated beside Sarah, she watched as their vehicle lumbered carefully down the corduroy sideways ramp. On the hard-packed sand they began to move swiftly. The waves were crashing and tumbling in an ocean more violent than it had been when Mr Torrens had brought her down. She mentioned this to Sarah, who answered:

'Yes, it's only to be expected. It started blowing quite hard during the night. Didn't you hear it?'

'No, I slept the sleep of the just,' Nicola returned, grinning at the woman beside her, pushing away the memory of words spoken to her before that sleep of the just, and giving all her attention to this exhilarating experience; this swift rushing ride with a sun low on the horizon that sent its slanting, brilliant rays of light across an ocean, vividly blue between towering, white-capped waves. She pulled her jumper still more tightly about her and gave all her senses to savouring this golden morning.

There was no doubt about the speed. In no time at all they had turned in between the huge white dunes that appeared to guard the entrance to the beach and were travelling along the now familiar bush track. Nicola let her jumper hang loose. Now they were off the beach and away from the wind blowing across a thousand miles of sea, it was quite warm.

Their driver paid no attention to the spasmodic conversation among his passengers. He was concentrating on the very narrow track, often supplied, as Nicola had seen before, with only planks placed across washaways. Looking ahead some time later, she met his glance in the rear-vision mirror, and looked sharply away. He was her boss, that was all ... she wanted no further involvement.

The barge was on the far side of the river when they arrived, but even as they pulled to a stop, the unwieldy contraption began to glide slowly across. A low murmur of voices from the front seat came drifting back. At her side, Sarah was quiet, gazing out over the broad stretch of water with its low-lying mangrove-covered banks. Old cars, beach-bombs, they were called, were parked on either side of the landing stage. By the expression on the older woman's face, she didn't altogether approve of the ugliness these vehicles brought to what she considered her own region.

The barge edged into the bank, the planks dropped, and the Rover's powerful engine broke into a muted roar as it was driven slowly into its place. Mr Torrens poked his head round the back of their vehicle.

'Are you leaving us after all, Miss Grant?' he asked, smiling broadly at her. 'Hasn't our wonderful beach sunk its hooks into you yet?'

'I'm thinking about letting it do so,' she responded a trifle breathlessly, aware that there were more ears than his to hear her answer. 'I've decided not to sell my father's place, however. But for now, I'm going to work for Mr Huntly at the resort, and I'm going down to Brisbane to be ... outfitted.' She couldn't help her hesitation before the last words. She knew she wouldn't be uniformed like a slave-girl, but she had no idea what they would be like, and, she admitted to herself, she didn't like the idea.

The plump barge owner smiled, satisfaction showing as he walked back to the engine room. 'Well,' he said, 'I'm glad you're holding on to it. It'll be valuable later on.'

A hundred yards or so there was another stop, and helped out of the Rover, Nicola stood beside Sarah waiting for the next step of this journey of going to the capital. A mechanic backed out a large, plain grey car from the rear of the garage, but Nicola saw the crouching silver shape on its bonnet and knew that the trip to Brisbane would be as fast as the law allowed.

With no time wasted, they were quickly ensconsed in the back seat, Elspeth beside the driver. He turned round, saying, 'I'm going along the coast road, instead of the quicker inland highway, because I'd like Nicola to get an idea of our Sunshine Coast resorts.' He addressed Nicola herself now. 'You won't see much of them just passing through, but it's as well for you to have some knowledge about them. You'll probably get enquiries thrown at you once you're behind that desk. I'll add some literature from the city today, and you can look it over.'

Again Nicola told herself wryly that if she might have thought at any time she had been offered a job for other reasons than necessity, she could promptly disabuse her mind of any such idea.

Leaving Tewantin and its twin town, Noosaville, behind, they flew along a coast road; the blue, tumultuous ocean always there, although craggy headlands, rock-strewn, sometimes took over from the beautiful silver-sand beaches. The sing-song, exotic names of settlements that sped behind them made music on her lips: Cooloola, Peregian, Coolum, Caloundra....

Sarah's voice came from behind her. 'I have a house on the Gold Coast, Nicola, south of Brisbane. Perhaps you'll be able to come down and visit when Candace comes home ... that is,' dryly, 'if Drew can spare you. Candace stays with me quite often in the summer.'

'Who is Candace, Sarah? She's been mentioned before.'

'She's Drew's young sister. He practically brought her up ... and practically again, I might add, almost in his own image. He really is clever, that Drew.' The expertly coiffured head next to her was shaken in admiration for the man in front of her. 'Their parents were killed when she was only eight, and she must be almost nineteen now. But Candace is sweet ... and charming, in spite of having more than her share of this world's goods. She could have turned out so differently.' Nicola wondered if her companion's eyes rested contemplatively on Elspeth Percival while she was speaking.

'They're very close, she and Drew,' Sarah was continuing. 'I only hope they each like whoever the other marries.' Again, and Nicola was sure this time, her glance rested on that beautiful woman in front of them. Nicola also remembered a voice saying in a dim hurricane lamplit room, 'I have a sister of your age and you'll be coming, one way or another.'

Sarah was lying back, silent now, and she did likewise, as the big car ate up the miles; pleasant miles, Nicola decided, gazing out of the window at the blue and golden day. The voices of the two occupants of the front seat were audible, with occasionally a laugh echoing through to the rear; sometimes it was a gay high tinkle, then would come a low deep chuckle. Suddenly, out of the blue, the owner of that deep chuckle turned unexpectedly, catching her gaze upon him.

'Brisbane coming up, Nicola,' he told her. 'We're in the outskirts now. We're going to diverge a little to drop Sarah, so you'll be entering the capital in a roundabout way.'

Gradually the traffic thickened and buildings began to rise to the sky. Before a large apartment block, Drew pulled into the kerb, stepped out to carry Sarah's case, and was returning immediately, laughing over his shoulder at either her or someone beyond.

In the heart of the city he found a parking space, fed the meter, then opened the back door. 'Come along,' he told her, 'and we'll see what Mrs Croft can find for us.

'I've brought you someone else to dress for me, Mrs Croft,' her employer was saying to a middle-aged, perfectly turned out woman, who came down the long carpeted room to meet them. 'This is our new receptionist, Nicola Grant. Do you think you'll be able to fix her up with some of our yellow uniforms to match her job— the kind with epaulettes like Peter's?'

The reply when it came didn't concern Nicola. 'I'll have you know, Mr Huntly,' the salon owner informed him, 'that I don't understand how the word yellow can be associated with any of my creations. Would you be referring to that special Golden Citrus material I found for you?'

There was a gleam of a smile in his eyes, Nicola thought, fighting back a grin herself, and he half bowed to the tall figure facing him, her expression so complacent. 'Right you are then, I stand corrected, but can you have some dresses ready for around three o'clock. God, woman, that leaves you almost six hours!'

A sound suspiciously like a snort came across to Nicola, standing between these two antagonists. Drew just stood there and waited.

'All right, I expect I might be able to,' the reply came crushingly. 'But it'll cost you, don't forget.'

The man merely shrugged, grinning. 'I'll leave her with you, then,' he exclaimed, and turned to Nicola. 'I'll pick you up here for lunch about one o'clock or thereabouts. Could you amuse yourself shopping in Queen Street after Mrs Croft has measured you ... or whatever it is she does? But don't go getting lost. It's a strange city to you, so take care. Do you hear me?' The last few words were curt.

'Yes,' she answered him mockingly, an employee to an employer, thinking of his words to her last night. *They* were certainly not employer's words. Rape indeed! And in her own bedroom too! But, 'Yes,' she repeated, 'I'll do some shopping and I'll be back here at one o'clock.'

She received a sharp look: a raised eyebrow, but he merely said. 'I'll leave you to Mrs Croft's tender mercies, then, and get about my business.' With a half-raised hand in salute he was gone.

Watching his back disappearing down the long room, Nicola suddenly felt a pang of abandonment. So many things had happened in the last week since she had been told of her father's death. She had had to realise that despite having no contact with him, there had still been someone belonging to her on this earth, now.... She straightened, shrugged. She was quite capable of taking care of herself.

As she measured and pushed around, Mrs Croft spoke only to give her junior assistant instructions. Glancing at this young girl as she was twirled around at one time, Nicola received a wide grin. She was about Nicola's own height, but this was all the similarity that existed. Dark curly hair, clustered close to her head, and she wasn't thin, she was angular. Also unlike herself, Nicola thought a little wryly, confidence and self-assertion seemed to make up a considerable part of her stock-in-trade.

Material was fashioned and pinned upon her, lengths were ascertained, widths commented upon, and it was in an incredibly short time that Mrs Croft, sticking the last pin away, told the two young girls, 'There, that should do.' One further encompassing glance, and she added, 'Finish it off, Naomi, then make tea. I'll be at my desk. Perhaps Miss Grant would like a cup too. It's been a long session.'

Amazed at this breaking down of so formidable a frontage, Nicola said only, 'Yes, thank you,' when really not wanting to stay at all. She glanced up to see the young assistant winking at her.

As she was shown into the back premises, her interested gaze went around it as Naomi switched on a kettle, before proceeding with material and patterns through a further door, which swung back to allow through the sounds of machines.

'There, that's the beginning of your uniforms,' she grinned at Nicola as she returned. 'Coo, but your boss is a lot of all right, isn't he? I wish he were my boss for a few hours.' She took in the look on Nicola's face, and giggled. 'Don't look so shocked,' she said. 'Don't you think he's a bit of all right, too?'

Really at a loss as to what she should answer, Nicola took shelter in subterfuge. Certainly she was unwilling to discuss her newly acquired employer, but this girl before her would require some kind of an answer. She said, 'I expect he could be called attractive. I only think of him as my employer, however.'

The tea made and a tray carried through into the salon, Naomi handed Nicola her cup. She sipped at the scalding liquid and ventured a question.

'Naomi?' then continued at receiving a nod of acquiescence, 'I thought I might buy a couple of dresses—one for the afternoon, and a short one for special evenings. My Cairns wardrobe could do with some replenishing. Do you know any shops? Not this sort—I should imagine that clothes from here would be beyond my budget.'

'Too right they would. You have to have the hard loot to shop here, and you don't look as if you belong to that lot.' Naomi was running an expert eye over every stitch Nicola was wearing. She added, 'No, those clothes wouldn't compare with the sort Madame Elspeth buys here.'

Naomi shoved the remainder of a biscuit into her pert, gamine mouth, and, striking an attitude, began to walk and gesture about the cluttered room. Almost against her will, Nicola found herself doubled up with delighted laughter. It really was Elspeth to the life! She wondered what that haughty miss would make of being taken off in such a fashion by someone like Naomi.

'Do you know her, Naomi?' she asked, still smiling widely.

'Actually, not to say know. But she buys her clothes from Mrs Croft. And of course it was she who brought your boss here to have these uniforms made.

'But about your dresses—I do know a small boutique that should have something to suit you. Not really cheap, but not outrageously expensive like here. And they have good stuff. I'm off at twelve o'clock. Would you like me to meet you, at the GPO, as you don't know Brisbane, and we'll see what we can come up with.'

'Why, yes, I'd like that, Naomi. But I have to be back here by one o'clock to meet Mr Huntly.'

'That'll be okay. All these places are within cooee distance of one another. I'll give them a ring telling them what I might think would suit you, so they can have something out ... I know your measurements and your probable price,' she continued, and laughed outright, as Nicola made to interrupt. She was completely uninhibited, thought Nicola, undecided whether to take offence or accept her, warts and all. She did the latter.

'So long as you do, then. I certainly can't pay what

Elspeth probably does. And yes, I expect after that session in there,' she threw out a hand behind her, 'you'd know my size. You won't be giving up your lunch, will you?' she added somewhat anxiously.

'No ... all in a day's work. I'll see what you think of my pick for you. Every facet of the rag trade is meat to my grinder, you know,' continued this incalculable five-foot-two gamine she had just met. 'I'm going to own a salon like this myself one day,' Naomi tacked on, as she reached for Nicola's cup to run it under the tap with her own.

She would too, thought Nicola.

'Still, that's in the future. I'd better get a move on right now in the present. Today's one of our busy days. I'll see you at twelve!' Nicola found herself out on the pavement without realising how it was accomplished.

Brisbane's streets and shops were like those of Cairns, only more of each, Nicola decided, strolling along, buying some things she decided she needed. Nearing the big General Post Office, she wondered if Naomi would actually meet her, someone she had just met a couple of hours ago. But even if she didn't know any special boutiques, Nicola decided, she could always go to one of the big department stores by herself and buy something there. Still, she would rather Naomi did her thing. She had great faith in her flair and judgment.

Loitering in front of the large sandstone building, glancing occasionally at the time, Nicola watched the world go by, and saw in all that crowded, hurrying throng not one interested or friendly glance flung her way. She could have been alone on a desert island.

However, it was a beautiful day. It was exciting to be in a strange, busy city. And she would have company for lunch, which she had tried not to think of. Then among that jostling, hurrying multitude, she spied one person interested in her. Naomi waved, her cheeky grin splitting her face from side to side.

Often, afterwards, knowing herself not to be easily led, Nicola wondered at the events of that day. Eventually finding herself outside Naomi's boutique, she hugged the more than solitary parcel close. She had the new afternoon dress she knew she needed, plus a lot of other items she knew she didn't. But most of all, and, her rare smile lighted her whole face, she had 'The Dress'.

It had been in a back room where all the fitting and buying, and outrageous suggestions from Naomi had occurred. The afternoon dress, brown floral motif overlaying shades of autumn apricots, would suit her colouring, and its round scooped neckline in the newest fashion sold her completely. She said yes as soon as it was brought out for her to try on. Also its price was quite within her budget.

However, 'The Dress' did not fall within the same category. She gazed from it falling from its hanger, up to the face of the assistant holding it, then across to the girl who had brought her here. She wanted it! She asked the price.

Before she could collapse, Naomi's voice broke in, laughing at her, 'What's a bit of money, Miss Grant, when something like that fronts you from the horizon? I knew it was here, it's the reason I brought you. Try it on!'

Of course Nicola tried it on. Shimmering, clinging, the blue-green of the waves before they broke on the shore at Teewah, she thought. It fitted as if made for her—with the exception of one part. Nicola pulled at the cleavage that exposed a line of bra on both sides.

'You'll have to wear it without one,' came from the the irrepressible Naomi. 'In fact, it was meant to show your shape. Your body in itself is all that's necessary under a creation such as that.'

'No, it is not! Actually, too, it's much too expensive—but it is beautiful, and I would take it except for the neckline. I couldn't wear that deep plunge. It's not my scene.'

'Naomi, slip into Vera's and get one of those newly designed bras. They have this colour. We'll see how it looks then. Take it off for a moment, Miss Grant.'

It still seemed skimpy to Nicola even over the garment Naomi was back with almost immediately. But heavens, it was lovely! She nodded. If she ever got to go out with anyone special—she didn't define who anyone special could turn out to be—it would impart confidence and an aura of expensive sheen.

Yes, they would take a cheque, they said. Nicola collected her little mountain of parcels, together with the precious box they handed to her, was taken outside and shown how to return to the salon. Naomi had already disappeared about her own concerns.

Arriving back at a minute to one o'clock, Nicola deposited her acquisitions on a shelf at the far end of the long room, which Mrs Croft indicated, then returned to wait just inside the front door.

Watching the flow of pedestrians pass the dress salon entrance, Nicola saw Drew as he crossed with the lights; picking him out even among all the passing parade. He paused in front of her and smiled.

'Punctuality is one of your virtues, I see,' he remarked, taking hold of her elbow and walking her outside, then he added, 'Have you any parcels?'

'Yes, but I've left them with Mrs Croft. I'll collect them when we call for the uniforms this afternoon.'

He directed her steps to a side-street, helped her into the Jaguar, and said casually, 'We're going up to the Terrace. Okay?'

Any place would be okay with her on this golden afternoon, she thought, watching him wend in and out among the busy traffic. Nicola could drive, but she shuddered at the thought of driving among this chaos. Abruptly he swung the big car into a parking slot much too narrow for it, and grinned down at her. 'Lucky, wasn't I?'

She let her breath out slowly. She didn't know about luck: she had been waiting for the noise of grating metal. Where they had parked was no quiet backwater, either; a stream of cars going both ways was like a perpetual moving assembly line. After feeding a parking meter, her companion clasped her firmly by the arm, and in a break in the traffic she was whisked across the busy roadway, a few steps along the pavement, and through big glass doors.

They entered a lift which slid silently, smoothly up; doors slid open and she found herself actually in the restaurant. Directed to a table, she took the seat held for her and glanced around. She was sitting beside a sheet of plate glass, and so high in the sky that she could see over the whole city.

'Would you like me to order for you, while you enjoy your romantic view?' her companion's voice asked.

Had he put emphasis on the word romantic? He had used it about her before, she remembered. She didn't care. She was just going to sit back and enjoy each event as it came.

'All right now, Nicola.' Drew swung round after the waiter he had been conferring with moved away. 'Enjoy your lunch, but as we're in the same line of business, you might take note. The service here is known to be excellent. At our own place I would like that to be the impression too. A lot of the clients we'll be catering for will expect no less, but with the added bonus of complete relaxation.'

And Nicola did enjoy it all, both the food and the company, though she had decided that she had better watch her step with the latter. She was not unused to eating out occasionally. She had partied, and danced, and barbecued, up north; the environment of her working life had abounded with attractive professional men, but this man beside her was different as far as she was concerned.

As they plummeted swiftly to ground level after leaving the restaurant, Drew informed her, 'We'll collect those uniforms and head for home, and we'd better slip along too,' he had pushed up a cuff to glance at his wrist-watch. 'I want to get out of the city before the rush-hour starts, or we could be held up and miss the tide.'

As they walked the short distance to cross to the car, a voice interrupted, shouting, 'Nicola—hi, Nicola!'

She swung round, her foot slipping on the kerb. She fell ... and there came a screech of brakes, the sound of a horn echoing stridently. Drew's face, inches away, not half as tanned as she remembered it, loomed above her, and she was picked up and swung to safety.

Setting her down, he raised a hand to the large vehicle that had missed her by inches and waved it on, then hurled round to the driver of the red sports car, long, low-slung, who had called to Nicola. It had moved out of the tangle of transport and was parked on the far side of the road: its owner, waiting a break in the traffic flow, ran across.

CHAPTER FIVE

'GOD, Nicola, I thought you were a goner!' the young man, tall, black-haired, brown-eyed, the answer to any maiden's prayer, exclaimed. 'I'm sorry I shouted, startling you, but I couldn't believe my eyes. Dad didn't say anything about you not being up there with him ... you were still there in Cairns when I came back from the holidays.' He glanced from her to her companion, then gazed more sharply at the man glowering at him. Very seldom was Gerry Redfern glowered at.

Shaking a little, even dazed a little, at the close shave she had had, Nicola put out a hand. 'Gerry...' she said, and turning a little in the arm still holding her, she tried again: 'This is Gerry Redfern, Drew. His father is ... was ... my boss in Cairns. He's down here at the university. Drew Huntly, Gerry.' Suddenly, so unexpectedly, she started to giggle. God, she thought, is this what they mean when they talk about shock? She really didn't intend to laugh, it just suddenly seemed so funny to be saying, 'And this is my boss now, Gerry.' But somehow it came out.

Abruptly, it was at her now that Drew was glowering. 'You're shaking,' he said sharply. 'Are you sure you're all right? Look, we'd better get over to the car, and then maybe to a doctor.' He reached into a pocket, withdrawing a card. Handing it indifferently to the young man looking so anxiously at Nicola, he told him:

'My address and phone number. Call me some time. I want to get Nicola away from this bedlam,' a throwaway gesture indicated the busy roadway, and arrogance wasn't the word for his attitude.

'But I want to talk to Nicola, I want to find out.... Have you left up north, Nicola? Are you living down here now? I'd like to get in touch....' Anger began to meet Drew's indifference, but it produced no results. Nicola was being turned towards the crossing, words coming over her companion's shoulder. 'You have my number, ring some time. I'll put you in the picture.'

Leaving a frustrated young man who was doing the glowering now, they crossed to where the Jaguar was parked.

'I'm sorry ...' she began from the seat where Drew had desposited her. 'I was stupid, slipping like that, but it's all right now, shouldn't we be going? I don't want to be responsible for missing that damned tide.'

'You should really see a doctor, I think I'd better....'

In her urgent desire to stop him she put out a hand, grabbing at his. It lay there, warm, strong, and a current passed from it.

Fingers turned, clasping firmly. Silence, absolute, reigned in the little world that enclosed them on a busy street. Nicola raised her eyes to find Drew's face so very near. His eyes, hooded, only half seen, gazed into hers, and she knew with certainty that she was going to be kissed. She felt her own lids fall lower as she sensed those chiselled lips come closer. Then suddenly a shadow was across them both and a voice said:

'Is she all right? I was getting out of my car and saw the accident. I'm a doctor.'

Nicola's eyes had opened with a jerk, and she heard distinctly the smothered expletive that issued from under the breath of the man beside her; but as he prepared to emerge and speak to the stranger, his tone was pleasant, grateful.

'Thank you, but she says everything is normal. I don't think the car touched her, but would you advise going to check with a doctor?'

Nicola felt her wrist taken in cool fingers, and impersonal, professional eyes looked her over. She remained quiet, till those assessing fingers had gone, and heard the doctor saying, 'She appears to be quite all right. Perhaps a little shock. Put that rug around her,' he pointed to a plaid travelling blanket folded on the back seat, 'and put her to bed when you get home.'

He listened while Drew explained that they were going to Tewantin and from there up the beach, then remarked again, 'Just keep her warm and relaxed. Stop when you can and have a cup of tea—hot with plenty of sugar. I think that's all.' He turned then, brushing Drew's thanks aside, and walked away.

Again Nicola watched her companion slide into his seat, and again he made no attempt to start the car, leaning across the back of the seat to pick up the rug. Taking no notice whatever of her protest that it was summer and quite warm, he shook out the folds of the blanket as well as he was able, and leaning right over her, tucked an end around her shoulder nearest the window, patted it carefully under her chin, to fold the other end in behind her on his side. Glancing down then to see that it enveloped her to her feet, he exclaimed, 'There, that should do it. Keep it on!' The last sharply, as she moved, not intending to dislodge it, but merely to straighten one arm which had been caught too tightly.

She answered him, if not sharply, at least with exasperation. 'I wasn't going to push it off, but I feel so silly sitting here wrapped up, like an Indian papoose, on a day like this. People will think we're mad if they glance in and see us.'

'They can think what they like, I couldn't care less,' and the tone of his voice showed that fact absolutely. What people thought, she realised by now, wouldn't concern Drew. They were in the traffic going through the city as he finished speaking. Finding a parking spot he slid out and was gone without another word.

She looked out over the thronged pavement and caught more than one amused, interested, or plainly astonished glance, and wondered idly if Mrs Croft would give Drew the parcels she had left there this morning. Somehow she couldn't care if she did or not, then Drew was standing at the back of the car, sliding an armful of boxes and parcels on to the seat. A head capable of only half turning within its straitjacket saw that her morning's shopping was among them.

The door was firmly closed, and it was getting a familiar sight to see him slip into a car in the particular way he used. She also decided, as she glanced swiftly at the profile facing her, that she would not let her imagination run away about that little episode upon the terrace. She had been around enough to know that men liked to kiss girls, with no other thought in their minds but the pleasure it gave them. She didn't like being kissed for kissing's sake herself, but she realised that Drew would not have known that, would not have known either that for the first time in her life she had desperately wanted a man to kiss her.

She lay back in her cocoon and watched the main street of the city slip by, noticing when the car turned off and began to edge along what must be warehouses, then pull sharply into a vacant parking lot before a huge sombre building. She was asked somewhat anxiously if she would be all right here, as he would probably be a while inside. It was with more than a little acidity that she replied:

'Of course I will! I'm a perfectly normal, healthy girl, and all I've had is a small shaking up.'

Her companion's lips tightened, but he only wound up the window and locked it—as if someone might come along and abduct me, was the ironical thought that drifted through her mind.

Reappearing, he was accompanied by a workman, both carrying large cartons which were stowed without loss of time. The big car was soon snarling through the afternoon traffic which was beginning to build up to peak hour proportions.

Out of the city and along the highway travelling north, Drew turned the speeding car off into one of the large garage-motels. They had not long to wait for the tea he ordered, after seating her at one of the attractive small tables. He poured the liquid himself when it came, adding some half a dozen cubes of sugar into one of the cups before handing it across to her. Overruling her protest, he merely said, 'It's what the doctor ordered. Drink it!'

Nicola tried to drink it, and it did go down, albeit slowly. And handing back the empty cup, she admitted she really did feel better.

As they began to climb the range road of the Buderim mountain, Nicola's eyelids began to droop and the country unfolding before her gaze started to blur and run together. She didn't know that her companion, after glancing once or twice at the motionless figure in the corner seat, the furrow between his eyes growing more pronounced, searched for a safe place along the climbing road to pull in. He reached out a hand, and with the back of his fingers touched her cheek. For a hot summer's day it was remarkably cool, and his hand slid down to one of the limp wrists lying so slackly on the top of the rug he had still insisted upon when leaving the café. Somewhat reassured by the steady pulse-rate, he carefully replaced the hand, and after another searching look slid back into his own place under the wheel.

Nicola was still sleeping at the end of the hundred-mile journey when Drew ran the Jaguar into the large echoing garage. After six now, it was still full daylight, although getting on towards evening shadows. He and the waiting garage-owner made short work of transferring all the paraphernalia they had carried back with them, and with a, 'Sorry to keep you waiting, Bill,' Drew opened the passenger door of the car.

Leaning inside, he gently shook the shoulder of the sleeping girl. She came awake suddenly, and for the second time that day gazed into dark grey eyes that were only inches away. This time, however, they held only concerned enquiry.

'Time to wake up,' their owner told her. 'We're on the last stage home.'

Suddenly, blindingly, in her just awakened state, Nicola knew that this was what the beach had become to her in the so short time she had been back ... this land of tomorrow, that was hers, now, today.

'Yes.' She took hold of the hand held out to her, and was swung up into his arms, and this time he completed the action he had contemplated before. His head came downwards, but not before his voice, soft, teasing, half-laughing, had said:

'You look like a baby girl, just awakened out of a sleep to be kissed goodnight—and of course a baby girl mustn't be disappointed.'

It was the merest fleeting kiss ... a butterfly caress; his lips resting with the lightness of thistledown, and it was Nicola who felt a sharp sense of disappointment when it was over. Then she was swung up into the front seat of the Rover, and Drew was beside her in one sliding movement, shifting packages to make enough room. Reaching down behind the seat, he brought up a quilted jacket and held it out.

At his look, she put it on meekly, while he waited before turning to the dashboard. The engine caught at the turn of a switch and with a hand waved in thanks to the man waiting at the big double doors, they were off.

They found the barge was also waiting to make its final trip of the day, and as they moved slowly across, Nicola gazed out over the wide stretch of water. Such a few short days ago she had made this same trip, she thought, but how greatly her life had changed since then. And it wasn't Mr Torrens this time that she watched manoeuvring the truck on to the planks stretching from the barge to the bank, and neither was it Mr Torrens who glanced at her and smiled as he remarked:

'Well, here we go. Hang on!'

It was an eerie sensation travelling through the bush at this time of the evening. The sun was low on the horizon, with very little of its light penetrating the ti-trees and indigenous scrub through which they were driving. Shadows lay long and ebony across both them and the thin snaking track. No sound at all was to be heard, only the noise of their engine broke the stillness.

'We might be the only people in the world,' Nicola

remarked unthinkingly, almost to herself, then looked quickly at the man beside her. He was concentrating on his driving, she was glad to note, and her gaze went out again to the weirdness of the landscape about them as it faded imperceptibly into dusk. It was a different matter entirely, the moment they had passed through the big white sand dunes on to the beach.

Life was there; fishermen trying their luck on the turning tide stood silhouetted in the afterglow which was quickly following the setting sun. Such a brief time it lasted. Now darkness was creeping over the whole world. Nicola was glad of her borrowed jacket, and sat hugging it about her, wide awake by now, enjoying the rush of wind as it swept against them.

And in the deepening darkness, the roar of the unseen waves from the other side of the driver seemed to gather in volume. She was glad of that solid presence who was sending the Rover flying over the wet hard sand that unfolded beneath the headlights he had just switched on.

Much sooner than she had expected, the vehicle swerved, and the sound of their passing changed, and she realised that they were on the ramp. Over the top and before the resort they arrived with a rush of motion, to be welcomed by the whole façade lit up like fairyland.

'Tell Jim to get these crates inside, Peter, and will you collect those other parcels in there,' Nicola heard Drew say as he helped her down the high steps, and, making their way inside, they were both brought to a full stop. Nicola, with pleasure in the scene greeting them: Drew, with an evaluating glance at all the new appointments the staff had been busy with.

Yesterday, the high-roofed public rooms had seemed a little austere, although charming and airy, bestowing a sense of space. Now they presented an enchanting picture. They were curtained, and sparkling heavy ash trays gleamed from the small intimate tables scattered about. Huge pottery containers stood waiting to be filled on the morrow for the opening. Catching Mrs Hill's glance, Nicola followed her as the older woman turned and walked through to the dining room.

Here the change was even greater. She noted tablecloths and napkins of the same Golden Citrus as her uniforms: gleaming silver and shining glass. Motifs with Australian connotations adorned the walls, and were present in the heavy drapes at the windows. She met Drew's gaze, and an eyebrow went up.

'You like it, apparently, Nicola. I hope others share your sentiments tomorrow when this room is full.' He turned from her to the woman by her side, saying, 'It looks well, Mrs Hill. You and the girls have my compliments! Get some wine from Peter, and drink to the success of the place at your dinner tonight. Now, Nicola, off you go. Have a hot shower and get to bed.'

She began to protest, but meeting those grey, unsmiling eyes, closed her mouth.

'She almost got herself run over,' her employer answered the unspoken words but astonished look of the housekeeper—whoever thought of going to bed at seven-thirty at night? 'Tomorrow,' he was adding, 'I want everyone on their toes, so off to bed with you, Nicola, and get a good rest.'

So, making her way to the back exit, Nicola walked slowly along to her unit, hearing through her preoccupation the crash and breaking of the wind-propelled waves. It certainly was a wild night tonight. Dropping her handbag on to the dressing table, she went through into the bathroom, and turned on the taps. The hiss of water striking the tiled enclosure followed.

I'm really not going to bed right away, she thought, whatever anyone says, but she knew she would enjoy a long hot shower. In her nightdress, she stood brushing her hair before the looking-glass, ends on forehead and nape wet from the condensation of prolonged exposure to steaming water.

But it wasn't her own face she saw reflected back at her. It was dark grey eyes before they became close ... so close. Drew had intended to kiss her, she knew, before that doctor had interrupted them. And she had wanted him to ... she knew that too. But now she wasn't in shock, and she remembered her vow not to become involved.

She shrugged, kicked off her scuffs and climbed into bed. Taking up a book from the bedside table, she left it lying idly in her nylon-covered lap, but looked up when a knock on the door preceded Glynis, one of the waitresses, who carried a covered tray.

'Here's your dinner, Miss Grant. Mr Huntly said

to bring you something light. He'll be in later to see you.'

Over my dead body, he will, thought Nicola, moving to accommodate the tray being placed across her lap. She said only, 'Thanks, Glenys, but tell Mr Huntly not to bother. I'm perfectly well, and I'm going straight to sleep after I've eaten.' There, she thought, that should keep him away!

When the girl had departed she ate a little, left the rest, then pulled the cosy-covered silver pot nearer. She discovered it was not coffee, which she had expected, and wondered who had realised that tonight she would prefer tea.

Pouring the hot, fragrant liquid, she added milk, and, with an inward shudder at this afternoon's additive, a mere half-spoon of sugar. She was lying back against her banked-up pillows, savouring it, when another knock sounded. Someone coming for the tray, she thought, as she called for them to come in. She jerked upright as her employer entered.

'Oh!' was all she could manage.

An eyebrow went up and a glance took in the tray on her lap. 'Good!' he exclaimed. 'At least you've eaten some dinner.' A grin, not a smile, suddenly tugged at the corners of his mouth as he continued. 'Are you enjoying the tea? I thought you might prefer it, to make up for what you had to drink this afternoon. But doctor's orders are doctor's orders, you know.'

He had been running his glance over her as he spoke—only checking her health, she knew, but suddenly his expression changed, and abruptly she wanted to be out of bed, a dressing gown over the revealing nightdress, standing up to meet this new threat.

Quickly she swung her legs over the bedside, and standing, gazed across at the chair with her dressing gown flung across it.

'Oh, come on, Nicola, don't be silly!' His eyebrow had climbed to incredible heights. He walked over and swung her up into his arms, impersonally, casually, to deposit her back from where she had slid. Leaning over, both arms holding her captive between them, he withdrew a hand to straighten up.... It trailed across legs left bare from a rucked-up nightdress, and brought a new dimension into the periphery of area containing them. She saw the start, the hesitation.... Drew hung, half suspended above her, and from wide open, startled eyes she saw his head come low, blotting out the single stream of light the room held; only a shadow on the far wall showed a reading lamp was burning.

She wasn't kissed, however. His lips went lower, resting in the deep cleavage disappearing into the fragile nylon and lace; then they drifted to move sideways to the white elevation of raised flesh at one side.

Lids drooping over closing eyes, she felt his mouth move, but again his lips bypassed hers. They rested first on one closed eyelid, then on the other. But suddenly they had changed position again. She was being kissed now, and without any will, any knowledge of doing so, her arms went up to clasp behind his neck.

Through the thin, delicate material, she felt his hand

in the small of her back press her closer, fusing body to body. Experiencing the blaze of passion engulfing them, she knew what was happening ... she felt the heartbeats against her breast like galloping hoof-beats, but she didn't care ... she didn't care....

She was thrust back into reality abruptly. Her eyes flew open to look into his, not grey, but black ... blazing, and dark.

His sharp indrawn breath reached to her; the expletive hard between clenched teeth, then his body was across hers no longer. He swung round, and stood with a hand gripping the chair back. What a thing to notice at such a time, she thought, not even knowing she was thinking; the knuckles were white, clenched about the wood. They unclasped, and he walked away from her towards the bathroom. She heard a glass clink against the shelf as it was removed and then the noise of water gurgling from the tap. He returned, a glass of water in one hand, the other shaking out some tablets from a small glass phial. He stood beside the bed, close, looming over her, and held out both hands.

Making no attempt to take the small white pellets, she gazed up at him. 'I don't take tablets. Please....' she added, catching his expression. 'I really don't need anything.'

'I brought them for you before....' His words trailed away, only to resume, 'Now come on, Nicola, swallow them. You needed them before ... you need them more now.'

Still she made no effort to reach for them. But words

came to her, soft, silken, and she recalled someone saying that it wasn't when Drew spoke loudly that he had to be watched. The time to take cover was when his voice dropped to softness.

'One way or another,' the silken voice was saying, 'and I remember using these words once before to you, you are going to swallow these, so which way is it going to be?' He placed the water on the bedside table and an arm came under her, supporting her shoulders. 'Now,' that soft voice went on, 'be a good girl and put these in your mouth.'

They were in her mouth before she knew she had taken them, and she drank from the glass he held for her. He then set this on the dinner tray, lifting it from the very edge of the bed where it was tilting dangerously upon the rumpled coverings. He placed it upon a chair and turned back, looking down at her.

'Well,' he said curtly, banked-up voice held in check, 'I'm not going to say I'm sorry ... I'm not. I'm going to warn you not to get any ideas about leaving, because you won't be. Goodnight!' He was gone, closing the door softly behind him.

CHAPTER SIX

A COMMOTION was making a hell of a noise. She wished it would cease, but it kept going on and on. From the deep unconsciousness into which she had fallen at long last, she drifted upwards, and suddenly was awake. She recognised that it was Jim knocking at her door as he had done yesterday. She must get an alarm clock, she decided absently, and then, abruptly, the memory of last night penetrated and any absentmindedness departed.

'It's seven-thirty, Miss Grant!'

'Yes, okay, Jim, I'm up now, thank you.'

Those tablets Drew ... no, Mr Huntly, she vowed, had given her last night must have been strong. She still felt whoozy. Drew.... Pushing the thought of him away, Nicola set about opening drawers on her way to the bathroom. Showered, she paused beside the chair on which the two boxes from Brisbane still remained unopened, and untied the cord from the larger one. Pushing aside tissue paper, she lifted out the top uniform. The material was lovely, so was the colour. She laid it aside and swiftly selected a straight, tight skirt and a white silk sleeveless blouse, with a tiny frill around the neck. Yes ... she gazed at herself in the mirror. Yes, she thought again, she looked like a working girl groomed for a day in the office. Kicking off her scuffs, she donned low-heeled white sandals and, opening the door, stepped outside to start her new life.

It was a beautiful day on which to begin it, too, she decided, as she walked the small cement path to the back entrance. Entering the kitchen, she was glad to see just the person she was looking for.

'Mrs Hill,' she begun, 'what do I do about meals now that I've started work? Will I just get my breakfast here and take it to the staff dining room, and would you tell me where I should sit?' She threw out a hand towards the room opening off the kitchen.

'You're to eat with Peter and Mr Huntly, my dear. Go along now and sit where you did before, and one of the girls will see to you.'

Having no option, Nicola went along, knowing she would much rather have had her meals in the staff dining room. Still ... she shrugged, and walked sedately into the big room where both Drew and Peter were at their table. They rose when she arrived.

'Good morning, Nicola,' Peter greeted her, and returned to his breakfast and his own thoughts.

'Good morning, Nicola,' said her boss, after a searching glance that took in the whole of her, then went back to the blueprints he was studying.

She thought thankfully that she needn't have been worried about having to be sociable, having to find topics to talk about, so she ate her meal when it arrived, poured a second cup of tea from her silver pot and drank it slowly, gazing over the view outspread before her. She didn't need company with her meals ... any company.... Ever moving, ever restless, always fascinating, the ocean provided enough of that.

Finishing her tea, she pushed back her chair and with a murmured, 'Excuse me,' made to leave.

'Wait a moment, Nicola,' Peter told her. 'I've finished, and I'll spend the next hour with you.

'Nervous?' he asked, when they found themselves behind the reception desk.

She didn't think so. This was a familiar environment, and the morning passed knowing she had everything pretty well at her finger tips. She placed the last pile of pamphlets on the side of her boomerang-shaped reception desk, and said to herself, That's that!

She liked the Australian Aboriginal motif that Drew had worked in through the whole resort. The public rooms were huge, airy, high-ceilinged, but in everything else that could be managed, he had worked in original Australian concepts. Stone, timber, art work, here! she moved a little to where she could see the Namatjira original that had only been hung this morning, probably crated in one of those cartons they had brought home last night. Last night.... She swung away from any thought of some parts of the previous night and looked instead at the big picture.

The painting graced the only wall without a break in it, and Nicola wondered if her employer had deliberately designed this room for that very purpose. A glowing jewel, it attracted every glance. She had hung in front of it the first time she had passed by this morning. The glorious colours, the strength, the limitless rightness of it, made it a focal point for an already charming room.

Absently, she wondered how Drew had come by it. Had he actually bought it for this place?—or maybe his parents had acquired it before Albert Namatjira died, and his paintings didn't cost the earth as they did now.

'Come along, Nicola, lunch!' Peter called. 'Only a scratch meal, though,' he added, 'things being how they are.'

She walked through to sit in the chair Peter was holding for her, and began eating the sandwiches already on her plate. Drew was there too. 'Hello, Nicola, fitting in?' he asked—in the casual sort of tone Peter would use, she thought acidly.

All right, she decided wrathfully, if that's how you want to play it, I'll play it your way. But you'll get no other chance to behave otherwise, ever again, I swear it. So, 'Yes, I think I am. You'd better ask Peter,' was all she answered.

Drew was buttering a slice of bread, giving to it all his attention. He did look up suddenly, however, and caught her watching him. His lids came down, hooding his eyes, but he said nothing else and began to eat his lunch.

They all made short work of the light meal, then Nicola was ordered by that inimical presence opposite her to take a couple of hours off, but to be dressed in uniform and behind her desk by four o'clock.

'Yes, certainly,' her expressionless voice answered. She left.

In her unit she opened the large suitcase which she had not yet properly unpacked, and brought to light two bikinis. Donning the older of the two, she twisted her long hair into a topknot before easing it into a rubber cap. She wanted no salt-impregnated head of unmanageable hair this evening. Making her way along one of the cement paths, she ran swiftly down the ramp to the beach.

For miles either way there was only the beach, lonely, farflung, with only blue tumbling waves creaming upon the silver sand. Then, gazing at the far horizon where deep blue sky met the just as deep blue sea, she realised that she had been wrong. There was a swimmer, and, she thought, whoever it was certainly had no sense. All she could distinguish was a head shooting the waves, and however good a swimmer he was, there were still sharks to be considered.

High-stepping over the first curling waves, she dived under as a big one broke. She was happy to swim and surf close in by the shore, but coming up from a long, low wave that she had ridden in to the shore line, she came face to face with that other swimmer. Grey-black eyes looked into eyes of ordinary blue.

'Was it you away out there?' God! Nicola put a hand to her mouth in dismay. Hadn't she intended never to address him personally again? He was her employer, that was all.

She heard him laugh out loud, his eyes glinting. As he put up a hand to brush the wet mass of hair from his face, his teeth showed, gleaming white in the dark bronze.

'Yes,' he replied, still grinning, 'that was indeed me. You have an objection?'

'How could I have any objection? No, I have none at all,' the words came coated with acid. 'I think it's a beaut idea you going so far out. Anything could be there! You might meet it!'

He laughed again, out loud again, too. 'As you say,' he told her, 'I could meet anything—great big hungry ones included. But really, I'm not stupid, you know, Nicola. I generally know what I'm about.' He was looking directly at her as he spoke, and the memory of kisses he had bestowed when presumably knowing what he was doing caused her to turn abruptly away. A wave loomed behind, and she rode it right up to the beach. He had apparently done the same, because he was beside her as she stood upright. As they stepped on to dry land, he enquired:

'Do you ride, Nicola?'

'Do I ride?' she echoed, the unexpectedness of the question causing her to answer him when she had had every intention of going straight to her unit. 'Yes,' she added.

His eyes got that dancing light that made a mockery of the grave face. 'What does yes mean?' he wanted to know. 'Does it mean you're a very good rider, just proficient, or can merely hold on to the reins?'

She gave sober thought to the question before replying, then, 'It means, I think, the second of your suggestions—just proficient.'

'God, you're priceless, Nicola! Don't you ever embroider or explain? Do you always search for the precise answer ...? Oh, never mind,' he exclaimed, continuing, 'The reason why I asked is that I have to go over to the homestead now, and I was wondering if you might like to come along for the ride ... if you did ride.'

She didn't want to go. Hadn't she vowed never to get within cooee distance alone with him, but words she didn't know she was saying escaped. 'What ... what about a horse?'

'We have such things as telephones—even in a primitive place such as this! Be in riding gear in ten minutes. We have to be back by four.' A hand-flicked dismissal, and he was striding along his own cement path.

In her own unit, Nicola pulled open her wardrobe door. She knew what she was going to wear—she also knew it wasn't glamorous. Still, it *was* suitable for riding. She took the much washed blue jeans from their hanger, but added a scarlet shirt for self-confidence. She dressed quickly and gave herself a final glance in the mirror. Satisfied, she saw that the scarlet showed up her blonde hair, bringing out golden lights, and undone low at the throat, the shirt had the new fashionable look. Jeans, of course, were jeans, she thought, struggling into them, but she knew her figure looked good in their tightness.

Outside, she came abruptly upon a man lounging beside some horses. A long wolf-whistle echoed among the buildings, and a faint pink mottled her cheeks as she met the gaze of the young man who had winked at her a few days ago.

'Oh, there you are, Nicola,' Drew's crisp voice echoed, 'and very nice too. This is Mike Pressler who practically runs the property. Come along.' He placed cupped hands for her to step into, and she produced the normal spring into the saddle.

'This is fairly even ground, isn't it, Mike? How about a run?' Drew asked.

'Yes ... if our beautiful blonde knows how to stick on,' he was answered, an impudent grin accompanying the words. It was a friendly gesture, none the less.

Oh, the hell with him, she thought. I'm not going to let him embarrass me. So, drawing a deep breath and an even firmer hold upon her reins, she grinned back in like fashion, and suddenly life was different. The breeze caught at them as they cantered along, streaming her hair in shining strands backwards. Powerful muscles communicated with her own, and she found she could ride naturally, able to guide her mount through the bush and trees straddling their path. Now she realised why Drew had asked Mike about the ground.

The sense of being a god flying along on a breeze

lasted for not as long as she would have liked. An interruption came, and Mike was off at a tangent. Drew turned his mount more slowly, and in a short distance they were on the outskirts of a mob of cattle. Mike was further over, down off his horse, working at something she couldn't see. A closer glance at the large beasts and Nicola began to edge her own mount nearer to her employer's.

These cattle seemed larger and heavier and more fierce than those she had been used to up north. Also, she didn't like the look, specifically, of one big animal that was eyeing her. Again she moved closer to Drew until she was almost touching him. A slight movement from his direction brought her glance from the creature whose attention seemed centred exclusively upon herself. He had that dancing glint in his eyes again, his face remaining grave.

'Surely you're not frightened, Nicola? Not you!'

There was a hint of asperity in the words that answered him. 'It's all right for you, Mr Huntly. You probably know them. I don't,' and, her attention on that huge lump of meat again, she added, 'And I don't know that I want to!'

He was reaching for her reins and was urging both horses into the midst of the mob.

'What on earth are you doing ... I don't want to go in there....' Her voice went high and wavery.

'I don't want to be called Mr Huntly, either. Sometimes in this world people have to compromise, you know. What is it to be—Drew, or the cattle?'

'You're mad!' she exclaimed, as her horse began to move again, then quickly, as the rough sides of the beasts began to close about her legs, 'You're mad, Drew, you have no right. . . .'

'That's fair enough,' his soft drawl answered, and with an expertise that showed ability and experience, she found herself beyond the milling cattle. It seemed also that they were about to resume their journey, because Mike regained his mount, and let out a yell that almost lifted her from her saddle. Then they were cantering leisurely side by side, and the rest of the ride was accomplished in silence.

'Here we are,' said Drew, and she saw his reins go tight as he pulled his mount to a stop. She was already on the ground in front of the homestead as he came to help her. Making no comment he took her reins and handed them with his own to Mike, guiding her up the wide shallow treads to the house.

Crossing a high-ceilinged verandah into its interior was like moving into a hitherto unexplored area. Polished floors with the gloss of centuries of rubbing reflected their passing, and turning a corner was a man coming to meet them. Old, weatherbeaten, he seemed the epitome of an Australian bushman.

'Hi, Drew.' His voice held the soft drawl that Drew's sometimes carried.

'Hello, Uncle Edward. I've brought Nicola Grant with me. She's our new receptionist.'

'Hi there, Nicola, nice to meet you,' she received.

She said 'Hi' too, and smiled, thinking it was a

beautiful room in which she was standing, but in the fashion of another age; not a modern object in sight. She wandered across to the window to stand with her back to it, gazing around. A finger lightly brushed an oval table beside her; heavy, on curved and sculptured legs. It was like touching silk, and like silk, too, were the carpets gleaming from their surrounding of polished wood.

Her glance went to the two men talking together. No wonder Drew's attitude was what it was, if this was his background, she thought—and thought too that they were not in the least alike, except for that tone they had in their voice sometimes. They turned at that precise moment, looking over at her, but it was the elder one who spoke.

'Tea!' Not a question, a statement.

'Only if it's quick, and we have it in the kitchen,' the younger one interrupted. 'I know you, Uncle Edward. With a young and pretty girl to put on an act for, you're very likely to make a ceremony of it, and we have to be back by four o'clock.'

'In the kitchen for today, then, but only on condition she comes back another time,' he was answered, and Nicola walked again across the lovely floor to follow in the older man's footsteps, feeling the younger close to her back as Drew came behind.

This was no room from another era. Today's sat on it completely—modern to its very door-jambs. Pale lemon walls, light golden benches, and gleaming yellow laminex confronted her. Crisp nylon curtains fluttered in the breeze from the long row of windows. She discovered Uncle Edward watching her and smiled in return, her rare smile, and didn't see the upraised eyebrow, the ironical smile, that came to take over the expression of the man behind her.

'I believe you only want to astonish people by the contrast,' she told this new friend, accepting what was being offered to her. 'And you succeed, indeed you do. In their own fashion, each is perfect. But you must have been here a long time to collect a room like the one we've just left.'

'Yes, we have. Sometimes too long, I think. We're quickly becoming an anachronism. That's the reason for this new venture. If it's a success, we might be able to keep this. And the world needs to be able to look into its past, as well as experiment with its future.'

He had been busy while speaking, and Nicola watched the spiral of vapour rise from the teapot before the lid was dropped upon it. Drew had taken beakers from a cupboard, and she saw that there were four. Biscuits were being placed beside them—not a common or garden variety, either, she noticed. Uncle Edward was doing her proud. He must have decided chocolate-coated marshmallow, and pink wafers, were more in keeping with young women. While the older man poured, Drew went to the door and called—no, yelled might be a more appropriate word, she decided:

'Mike!'

'Coming!' was an answering yell, with Mike following the echo. He came in, perched himself naturally on a high stool, and was as much a part of the group as was Drew himself. Nicola wondered what the people who had occupied that other room a hundred years or so ago would have thought of this phenomenon. Some of the changes time had wrought had certainly been for the good.

It was a pleasant quarter of an hour; casual talk, laughter that Mike provoked more than once ... last night's emotional episode might have been from another world. Then Drew was emptying his cup and running it under the tap, reaching for hers to give it the same treatment.

'We'd better be off, I'm afraid,' he said, 'or our guests will be arriving with no one to meet them, and that would never do.'

On their horses, after a final wave to the tall old figure leaning against one of the solid verandah posts, she spoke to her companion. 'He seems old to be your uncle, Drew. Was he a lot older than your father?'

'He isn't actually an uncle, more like a third cousin. What we've just left is a family property. He has grandsons my age, but they don't want to go on the land. As I'm an architect and have my practice in town, I have no expertise in cattle raising, either. I wouldn't have the beginning of Mike's know-how. He'll be the boss of the whole outfit one of these days.'

Nicola glanced across at the third member of the party. All she received from him was a grin—but an assured grin. A man of few words was Mike.

'The resort, however, *is* my baby,' Drew was continuing. 'And, speaking of babies ... come on!' He slapped his mount's rump in the same manner that Mike had slapped the cows, setting the three of them flying. They arrived at the resort, cantering, and, for Nicola, a trifle breathless. She found herself lifted down with no time lost, and faced towards her own unit. With a gay wave for Mike, and no more attention for the man who had just released her shoulders, she quickly set off.

CHAPTER SEVEN

BRUSHED shining fair hair, lightly made-up face, a Golden Citrus uniform, a last appraising glance ... Nicola let herself out of the room and walked to the back entrance. The whole place was deserted.

'In here, Nicola,' a voice called.

They were all gathered there, including the chef and his apprentice, the latter's surf-blonded hair catching at the eye. Peter threw a casual arm round her shoulders as he led her to the bar.

'What's it to be?' she was asked.

'Oh, something innocuous,' she laughed up at him. 'I wouldn't dare have anything else, seeing how important I've got to be and sound.' Her laughter died suddenly. Drew was looking at her from hooded eyes, his expression forbidding, and abruptly, Peter beside her, the casual arm about her shoulders was anything but casual.

She accepted the ginger ale he was holding out, and eased herself from the half-embrace. Glasses were raised. The toast was 'The resort'. The staff sounded happy, satisfied, Nicola thought as they departed kitchenwards. She didn't know if she sounded happy—she certainly knew how she felt.

Behind her desk, she checked again that everything she would need was where it could be got at—at a moment's notice. She tried not to think of her employer. And suddenly, almost immediately, the whole building was alive. Voices asking questions, people being led to their rooms—the first guests had arrived.

A second contingent was expected after work finished in the city. Nicola took the lone woman among this lot through to the lounge for a cup of tea, settling her at a table overlooking the terrace. Leaving her then to Glynis's ministrations, she returned to find herself still required at the reception desk. But it was Jim who was the most in demand, and Nicola watched his unhurried demeanour with admiration. He never seemed flurried. He handled alike suitcases, fishing gear, and the occasional peremptory enquiry.

Opening day! It was actually here. She sat on her high stool behind her boomerang barricade and smiled her social smile at a big jovial man as he crossed to go out the entrance door. Some confusion occurred, of course it did—this was the opening. But it was rectified quickly while time flew into limbo.

Called to a unit, Nicola saw that the lights were on as she returned, and soft music was sounding throughout the public rooms. Gravitating towards the bar and lounge, fishermen were clamouring for what comes naturally, and she saw that Drew was back from the trip he had taken down to the barge. Then, incredibly, the space before her desk was empty; opening day was a thing of the past.

'There, that wasn't so bad, was it?' On his way to the bar, Peter grinned the terse sentence over his shoulder.

Her smile in return was grim, however, as she shook back the hair from her hot face and cheeks. It mightn't have been not too bad, but it had certainly been hectic while it lasted.

The flap of her desk was being lifted, and Drew was behind the counter, standing close—too close for comfort, she reflected acidly. Why couldn't he keep his distance? Last night was last night. This was today ... cold unromantic daytime.

'That's over, thank God!' he was saying, adding, 'I thought at one stage order would never come out of that mad scramble. Aren't I lucky I decided that being alone in a beach shack was no place for a young girl, and came along and collared you.'

Nicola took up a pen and made hieroglyphics on a page of bookings, then feeling that she had to make some sort of a reply to the presence beside her, she said, 'It was only a job. I've had more difficult situations than today's to cope with in my time.'

Always afterwards Nicola thought that it was in that precise moment of time that there occurred the turning point in her life. From their first meeting there had been an unaccountable emotion in regard to this man. Passion too, now, with last night's lovemaking adding its own quota. But now she knew that if she never saw him again it would make no difference. This was a lifetime bondage.

Standing so close, within the periphery of the confined space behind the desk, magnetism, a force locking them, serious blue eyes looked into those above her; into eyes not grey but black, pinpointed with a brilliance that was hard to meet.

'Excuse me, miss....'

The man flung away.

Automatically attending to the guest's request, Nicola smiled him away, then turned to where Drew had been when that inopportune interruption had occurred. He was there no longer. She moved objects on the counter back and forth heedlessly, unaware of what her fingers were doing.

Time passed. She closed her desk and made her way to the dining room. Her meal finished, she walked past the terrace, seeing the little tables well patronised, then strolled to the top of the dunes for a breath of fresh air. It would settle her down before going to bed, she thought.

Just the white-capped waves showed in a darkness

that had only the stars to provide illumination. Raising her gaze, she swept the heavens. Yes, there it was. The Southern Cross blazed in all its familiarity up there in the star-studded arch above.

Turning, she faced the sprawling, brightly-lighted resort, then skirted it to make her way along one of the innumerable small paths to her own unit. Closing the door behind her, she leaned her back against it, memory crowding in; memory ... of kisses she knew she had more than returned ... of a body that had fitted to hers, flesh to flesh, curve to curve.... She drew in a sharp explosive breath. She had better begin to turn her mind to other things, if she wanted to get any sleep tonight.

Her uniform came off and she smoothed it carefully upon its hanger, then quickly set about the rest of her toilet. Flicking out the light, she pulled her window lever down to its furthest limit and climbed into bed.

Life went upon its normal way, fitting into a pattern that the succeeding days established. Nicola rose, dressed, then made her way to the resort proper. One morning, seeing all the holidaymakers eating out on the terrace in the sunshine, she said as Glynis came to get her order:

'It looks heavenly out there. I think I'd like to have my meal on the terrace too, Glynis.'

'Yes, well ... I suppose that will be okay, Miss Grant. It's just that we've had instructions you were to have all your meals at Mr Sinclair's table. Also, if he or Mr

Huntly are not around, we're to check with you if anything comes up. But you'd know that, I expect.'

'No, I didn't damn well know! And also I don't know if I like it. I certainly don't want the responsibility of a great place like this. You're not having me on, are you, Glynis?'

'I wouldn't dare have you on about such a thing. And anyway, we manage very well, we women, don't we?' Glynis gave her comfortable laugh and wended her way kitchenwards.

A chair being pulled out at the table brought Nicola's head swinging round and she saw Drew lowering himself into it. He gave her the customary good morning, and then became engrossed in what she saw was mail.

She drank her orange juice and poured her tea, wondering when he had got back. He hadn't been here last night.

He did speak then, as she was buttering her toast. 'Is that all you're having?'

Her glance rose to his: her reply was light, pleasant. 'Yes, it's all I ever have. I couldn't face a large cooked breakfast.'

'A cup of tea and a piece of toast seems hardly enough nourishment to work all morning on.'

'Well....' She allowed the sentence to trail off. She had no intention of changing her eating habits. Her companion raised his head sharply and looked directly at her, but forbore to comment and returned to his letters.

Nicola drank her tea and ate the despised toast, wishing she *was* outside, away from his presence. She rose as soon as she decently could, and left.

At the end of the second week, Drew went away, and Nicola decided that even though she missed him, thought of him, she was more content without his disturbing presence. She could eat a lot more easily with only Peter to share her meals—but she had added a bowl of paw-paw or diced pineapple to her breakfast. And that wasn't a victory for Mr Drew Huntly, either, she told herself.

He was away for almost a fortnight, then, glancing up casually from her accounts one afternoon, she saw him pass through the lounge. The impact of his unexpected appearance shocked her, and she took herself sharply to task for allowing such an emotional reaction.

He didn't have to come and say hello, she acknowledged. He had his own unit. She saw no more of him that afternoon.

Walking down towards the dunes, to watch as she sometimes did the fantastic sight of grown men—and important grown men, too—playing shuttlecock, she wondered where he had got to. Wishing he would materialise ... wishing he wouldn't. ... Peter had introduced the shuttlecocks, and Nicola had stared when the bats and shuttles had been produced one evening as the sun was lowering in the hinterland behind the resort.

'Don't you think they'll be used, Nicola? You'll see!' he had exclaimed, taking in her expression. And off he had gone down to the sands with Jim to fix the tall nets firmly. This evening, as she stood watching, she saw there were four 'courts' in use: the bats were flashing with incredible speed, the shuttlecocks flying back and forth. She conceded that it was a perfect place for the game, all the space in the world with no danger of crashing into any obstacle.

Along the edge of the creaming surf, casting from their long rods, men fished, entirely oblivious of lesser beings. Then there were what Nicola called the constitutionalists. Almost as if they were on an ocean liner, they marched, so far up the beach, then so far back again. Still, it was a lovely time of the evening, for any sort of activity. The sunshine was going; the bushland cutting off the fiery orb setting below the horizon at her back. The sand, both hard-packed brown and yielding silver, was in shadow. The sky, losing its brazen azure, was merging into a luminous arch of the palest blue. She grinned suddenly, catching sight of one of the men's faces as he bent to retrieve a shuttlecock he had missed. Stout, determined, and, by the looks of him, used mostly to getting his own way, he was going to hit the damn thing back, or know the reason why.

Moving a little to get a better view of a quite large fish one of the fishermen was reeling in, Nicola saw that someone else was doing the same thing. Drew had left a table on the terrace, and his line of direction would bring him to her.

He greeted her as if he had seen her only this morning, not almost a fortnight ago. 'It's in order for me to be down here, isn't it?' she remarked, feeling the need to be defensive. 'Peter knows where I am if he needs me.'

He looked her over, the smile gone from his face. 'I expect it is,' his reply was as curt as hers had been defensive. 'You wouldn't be here if you knew it wasn't. With the rave notices I've received from Peter about your ability, I imagine you can do pretty much as you like. Actually, I want it known to all the staff that that applies—within reason. This is to be a happy place.'

Nicola stood gazing at the creaming waves; a shiver went through her, and it was not the swiftly gathering shadows fast presaging the coming of night that caused it. A face, lovely, glamorous, was suddenly superimposed upon the scene before her, and not only a face; a whole entity was there, poised, and so assured. Elspeth's.

Because she had become accustomed to referring to him so, when addressing staff and holidaymakers in his absence, also maybe the memory of Elspeth providing an unconscious motive, she said, 'Yes, all right, Mr Huntly. I usually don't stay long, and I'm going now.' She felt herself gripped and swung round. The eyes above her were not hooded as they sometimes were, nor were they slate grey; they were almost black. The words, when they came, however, were soft, drawlingly slurred.

'I thought I warned you, Nicola. Though, after all, everyone is entitled to their likes and dislikes. But if you "Mr Huntly" me once again, so help me, be pre-

pared to take the consequences—and you may already
have some idea of the direction they might take.'

Angry herself now, feeling the rush of colour swamp-
ing her face, she tried to pull free. Seeing brute force
was getting her nowhere, she raised an eyebrow and
put disdainful indifference in her expression, as she
glanced down at the hand holding her arm. He spoke
again and the words came as softly as before.

'You may wipe that supercilious look from your face,
my competent little receptionist, because with me it will
get you nowhere. Now, what's it going to be? Trying
to get along together pleasantly—or being wilfully ob-
structive?'

Hearing that silken tone, that slurred bleakness, she
gazed up at him, wishing she had not started it, wishing all this unpleasantness miles away, and herself
safely behind her own familiar desk. But unerringly she
knew that she would have to do either as he bade her,
or she could leave this job.

'Very well,' she answered in a voice devoid of all
warmth. 'When I have to address you, I'll say Drew.'

'Nicola!'

But, her arm dropped, she had turned and walked
swiftly away. Behind her desk she subsided thankfully
on to her high stool, willing her legs to stop their trem-
bling. Should she have defied him and left this job?
She didn't want to. She loved the wide, windswept
beaches, the sound of the ocean as she went to sleep
every night ... the memory of a body fused to hers, of
kisses.... No, she would stay while she could.

Therefore it was with some trepidation that she went along to her dinner, wishing she could give the meal a miss, but not just being game to. Both of the men were in their places. They rose and saw her seated. She ate the food mostly in silence, and answered only when spoken to. Halfway through it, Peter was called away.

'It's just one of those things,' he answered Drew's enquiring glance, and departed.

Silence reigned in the oasis of their small table. She didn't know what to say, and apparently he didn't care. Then:

'You'll be having company on Thursday evening in your adjoining suite, Nicola,' her companion finally spoke. 'My sister is coming to spend some time with us.'

'Oh?' Quarrel forgotten, she smiled up at him, saying warmly, 'Is she? Sarah told me you had a sister. Her name is Candace, isn't it? What a lovely name to be called. How old is she? Is she like you?' As the last words tumbled out she came to a full stop. Drew was suddenly not looking at her. His head had lowered, his eyes hooded as they sometimes did.

But he answered pleasantly enough. 'I really don't know if she is—like me, I mean. I've never thought about it, but I shouldn't think so. I was coming to tell you about it on the dunes this evening, but I was diverted.'

What a way to put it, went through Nicola's mind, remembering the cold hostility with which he had spoken to her.

'She's going on nineteen,' he was continuing, 'and thinks I know nothing of what she wants, and what's worse, that I don't care what she wants. She's wrong. I only want her to be happy. She finished school almost a year ago, and has been touring England and Europe since.'

Heavens! Fancy, just like that. Touring England and Europe ... all those romantic-sounding places, Nicola was thinking, but she paid attention as Drew went on.

'I thought that if she saw something of the world, she might have second thoughts about making nursing her career, which is what she wants to do. Her grades weren't good enough for the university. Not that she isn't bright, she is—when it suits her to be. It just doesn't suit her to go to university. I wanted her to settle for a job in a doctor's surgery, a receptionist, like you, if she wanted something to do with nursing, but. ...'

She remained silent, not knowing what to contribute to this conversation.

'Candace is too young,' he was continuing, 'to be in contact with the seamy side of life that nursing would entail. Elspeth says that lots of girls like it. I don't want it for my sister, however.'

There it was in a nutshell. 'Not for my sister.' Nicola said slowly, 'I don't know Candace, but I do know girls who've taken up nursing. They probably might meet the problems of life sooner than those in other jobs, but I would imagine it would be the hard work that could be the drawback, not the distasteful aspects of the job. It's not the glamorous scene some young girls might think it.'

He grinned suddenly, teeth flashing in the brown face. 'Have you got thoughts, Nicola, that my sister is a little hothouse flower, tenderly sheltered from a cruel world? Well, my love, you were never more wrong. . . .' Nicola wasn't listening to the rest of his words. He had said . . . did he know what he had said. . . ? She caught the rest of his discourse. 'I brought her up to fit into this world of today, and I wouldn't have minded if she'd wanted to be a doctor like Elspeth, a children's doctor, as she likes children so much, but a nursing career . . . no.'

'I suggest you wait until you see her again,' said Nicola. 'She might not even want to do nursing now. Schoolgirls change their minds a dozen times. She may even want to stay here.'

'Here?' Drew shook his head decidedly. 'No, she won't. What would she do here? She couldn't take your place, and there's nothing else. Still, we'll see, and I expect we'd better get out of here; they're waiting to clear away.'

And so they were, she saw, and hurriedly rose to her feet.

CHAPTER EIGHT

AWAKENING slowly, Nicola wondered hazily what was the difference with the morning. She swung her glance to the small travelling clock on the bedside table; it was too early to wake up. Thursday, she thought. Oh, Candace was arriving this evening. She wondered what Drew's sister would be like, unable to visualise a girl who would look like him.

Warm, drowsy, thinking of him, of how her whole life had changed because she had decided to see the shack her father had left her, she turned restlessly on her pillow, her normal ability to come to terms with circumstances deserting her where he was concerned.

On her way to the kitchen for the first cup of tea of the day, she wondered if she could ask Peter for a couple of days off to go to Brisbane. Though she had mentioned it to no one, she would be twenty in four days' time. A twentieth birthday, she had always thought, was much more important than the old majority of twenty-one, or today's eighteen. One was suddenly out of one's teens, nineteen was so different from twenty. And it would be nice to go to the capital and maybe see a show, or do some shopping.

She drank her tea, and the day crowded in upon her. That was how it was here—busy sometimes, so that jobs fell over one another to be finished, slack at at others, with time on her hands. She gave lunch a miss, but an angry Peter ordered her out to the staff dining-room, where a bowl of soup and a plate of salad was put before her.

Later, glancing up from checking in a busload of southern fishermen, she saw two people standing before her desk. She looked from one to another; from Drew's light brown hair and sunhazed dark brown skin; from his smiling grey eyes and just as smiling mouth, to the girl beside him. She wasn't a scrap like her brother, Nicola thought in that first moment, but then Candace smiled saying warmly :

'Hello, Nicola,' and she was so greatly like him that the girl behind the desk was astounded.

'You don't need an introduction, I take it?' Drew's voice was saying, as she stood silent, gazing at them both. His words brought a faint pink to her cheeks, and she said hastily :

'I'm sorry. I was thinking you weren't a scrap like your brother, Candace, and then you spoke, and I had to have a rethink. Yet you don't speak as he does, and you certainly don't look alike.' It struck her unexpectedly. The eyes, it was the eyes ... the same, exactly, except that Candace's were made up, eye-lined and mascaraed, and very much shadowed. But her hair was as fair as Nicola's own, though straight and fashionably long.

'Yes, that's what they all say,' the younger girl laughed, a low musical chuckle. 'It must be because I've always imitated Drew. We're not really alike, except for our eyes, but everyone says we are.'

'Shall I take her along to her unit?' Nicola became the efficient receptionist. 'Will you just hold the fort here, please?' she asked her boss. 'We've been so busy, I simply daren't leave it. There's sure to be some complaint or other from that busload I've just checked in. I'll just take your sister up and come directly back, then she can get her unpacking.... Oh, God, how stupid of me! You'll want to take her up yourself, I expect. Here's the key,' she continued, holding it out.

Drew made no attempt to accept it. He took a few steps and the flap was lifted. Two hands were placed, one on either side of Nicola's waist, and she was swung round to face the small aperture; the voice above her head was saying:

'It's not my duty to take guests and/or staff hangers-on, to their quarters. Be off with you!'

Her fingers curled tightly over the rejected key, her waist still feeling the pressure of those fingers that had gripped, she remembered.... She went to stand beside the girl on the other side of the counter. Even in her confusion, she automatically checked for luggage, Drew told her:

'Jim has taken it up already. It will be outside the unit. Let Candace lug it in, she's strong and healthy, and if she must have all those cases, let her look after them.'

Nicola walked beside the newcomer, unlocking the door next to her own unit. Flowers she had arranged made the room fresh and welcoming and Candace moved round, exclaiming, showing her pleasure. She returned to the entrance, then, glancing ruefully down at the suitcases stacked tidily there.

'I'd better get some of these in,' she remarked resignedly, and as Nicola reached to help her, put out a restraining hand. 'No, you don't. Drew told me to do it myself. I'll be okay, Nicola, honestly ... you can go back with a clear conscience.'

Walking into the dining-room at her usual mealtime, Nicola received a shock. Drew, entering almost at the same time, and holding a chair for her, also pulled up short. Sitting complacently at a table just across from theirs, a grin on his face like a cat who had just consumed a whole bowl full of cream, was Gerry Redfern.

'Hi there, Nicola,' he called across. 'I told you I wanted to see you.'

She didn't even sit in the chair held for her: she stood, not knowing how to behave, then common sense coming to her aid, she went across, saying, 'Hi, yourself. What are you doing here?'

'I'm here for a fishing weekend. Isn't that what this place is for? If there's a bonus thrown in, like strolling on a moolit beach with you, I'll accept that too.'

Underground currents surrounded the two tables through the ensuing meal, growing more so after Candace made her appearance. Gerry's attention centred more and more on both girls. Drew just sat, his expression thunderous, but his glance rested on his sister, and Nicola wished Gerry would put a sock in it. Charismatic, assured, a satisfied smile on his handsome face, he flung tantalising remarks at them both from across his table.

She muttered to herself, 'That damned Gerry! He's just trying to be obstreperous,' and was profoundly thankful when Glynis bent over her with a message. She nodded and stood up, shaking her head at Peter.

Later, as she closed her desk which she had had to reopen, she caught up a light cardigan lying on a back shelf, wondering where Candace was; if she was with Drew, or Gerry. Informed by Jim that she had left for the beach already, Nicola joined Glynis and Mrs Hill and walked beside them down the corduroy ramp. It was pleasant just to stroll, not having to be bothered to make conversation. Drew was around: some distance off, certainly, but here ... the waves were tumbling in as a stiff ocean breeze sent them scattering, and towards the horizon the water shone silver, reflecting the moonlight in a million dancing points. There was laughter and a climate of ease of mind prevailing, but eventually there had to be the return home.

Asked to come along for a nightcap, Nicola politely declined, pleading tiredness. It was true, too. She was tired. It had been a hectic day.

She made her way around the side of the larger building and walked along the path to her own quarters. Inside, preparing for bed, she heard voices outside the next unit, Candace's and.... She lifted a corner of the curtain to glance out. The other speaker was Gerry.

As she watched, Candace laughed, and swayed towards her escort. Amazed, the watcher saw him not kiss the face lifted, but taking hold of a hand, press the expected kiss into it. Goodness, he had changed—or he was trying out a new technique. A scene formed before her eyes; in a far hotter climate than it was outside, though. But it also had taken place before a closed front door. Having no transport, she had gladly accepted Gerry's offer of a lift home. It had been a lively party, as were all the firm's Christmas staff get-togethers, and champagne as well as beer being the tipple, he had more than indulged himself.

She knew his reputation; the boss's son was fair game for gossip; but having known him from way back, she started by laughing at his determined amorous advances.

It was the laughter that had deterred him, that had made him angry, and it had taken more than a little diplomacy to soothe his ruffled feathers, but it had been that episode that had set the seal on their friendship.

Knowing him so well, she knew also that it had been Drew's high-handedness on the day of the Wickham Terrace accident happening that had made Gerry determined to find her. He could be as high-handed himself as Drew had been, but didn't like being on the receiving end of it. Nicola hoped he wasn't going to try anything with Candace; she shivered at the thought of Drew's reaction to any hurt his sister might suffer.

She shrugged, and continued with her undressing, and, in her nightdress, was brushing her hair into a shining cascade about her face when a knock came upon her door and Candace's voice demanded:

'Open up, Nicola. I want you!'

She went quickly to open the door, and fell back as the other girl threw both arms around her, giving her a swift hug. 'Come on, into my room, Nicola. Never mind being undressed, just shove on a dressing gown.'

'Don't be silly, Candace. I'm not coming out like this!' Nicola's voice held sharpness, but the younger girl grabbed a gown thrown across the foot of the bed and was dancing round its owner, holding it out, repeating, 'Come on, I want you!'

Nicola had no intention of participating in a heart-to-heart with Candace at this time of night. She had had a long day, and she was tired, but in the event she had no option; she was gripped by the arm and pulled out of her own door and through the one alongside it. Her own dignity made her walk naturally when she saw who was lounging on an easy chair against the wall.

He looked her over from the crown of her just brushed hair, shining, swinging free; the washed face, innocent of make-up, and, further, over the open lounging coat with the filmy nightdress beneath, in its see-through déshabillé. To, and this she had been unaware of till now, her feet, bare of any covering.

Bare feet were an integral part of this holiday place, she reminded herself, and her feet, even if uncovered, surely had no right to make her feel naked. She made her hands stay still, not allowing them to reach for the fastenings of her gown, and stood, hating that encompassing gaze raking her over. Her own glance slid deliberately past him, to rest upon the jumble and clutter upon the bed.

'Oh, thank you, Nicola.' Closing the door behind her, Candace turned an excited, radiant face to the girl she had just shanghaied. 'I'd planned to coax,' she was running on, 'to sulk, to threaten—oh, all sorts of things, and here it all falls into my lap. The one thing I want, and all because of you!'

Drew interrupted, his words brusque, almost cold. 'I expect Nicola doesn't know what you're talking about. Belt up, Candace, and calm down a little.'

If that tone had been used in addressing her, Nicola thought she would have curled up in a ball and crept away. Not Candace. She pirouetted in the confined space and sang in a nursery rhyme doggerel, 'I'm to go nursing, go nursing ... and it's because of you ... because of you, Nicola!'

This did cause Nicola to look directly at the man lounging so indolently there, but his sister was continuing.

'Drew says that if I still want to, I can try—with stipulations, though,' she laughed over at her brother. 'I have to promise that if I don't like it, I'm to tell him so, and not let pride stand in my way. I've promised!' She started dancing round the room again, apparently unmoved by that promise.

Nicola shook her head. She couldn't help it. 'I simply can't understand you, Candace,' she ejaculated. 'Just back from a fabulous holiday, able to choose anything you want to, carrying on as if you're about to go back overseas again, instead of having years of hard work before you....' A thought pulled her up. 'Why did you say it was because of me? I had nothing to do with it!'

'Oh, but you did, dear Nicola. Here was I, trying to find the present I'd brought back for Drew among all this,' she threw out an encompassing arm towards the jumble of parcels and clothes on the cluttered bed, 'and wondering how to broach the very subject. Then my darling brother asked if I would still like to do nursing.

'Talk about telepathy, I thought, but it wasn't. He told me you'd said you knew some girls who were nurses, and they seemed to be very happy, so....'

'I ... I never....' Nicola stammered. 'I ... I mean, you ... you can't let her go because of what I said.' She faced Drew directly. 'You can't let her do it because of me,' she repeated. 'Because I ... said....' The words trailed off when she saw he had no intention of replying.

Candace was also taking no notice of her worry, her efforts to get things into perspective. 'Look!' she was exclaiming, taking hold of the object in her brother's hand. 'Look at the wallet I brought back for Drew. Isn't the leather gorgeous?' she continued, stroking it lovingly. 'It has the City of London's crest upon it. I bought it for him because I loved London.'

'Stop babbling.' The man reached across as he told her this and reclaimed the wallet. 'I'm off. Get this junk cleared away and get to bed. You've come a long way today.'

Before Nicola could move out first, he was at the door. His sister flew after him. She stood on tiptoe and put her hands on his shoulders, reaching up to kiss his cheek. 'Thank you, Drew,' she told him softly. ''Night!' He was gone.

Bitter envy struck at Nicola. To be able to just casually reach up to Drew like that and.... She said shortly, 'I'm going too, Candace,' but lingered as the younger girl begged,

'Oh, not just yet. I'm too excited to sleep. Talk to me while I produce some order out of all this havoc,' gesturing towards the bed.

Helping to fold away blouses, sweaters, cobwebby lace, putting into drawers parcels labelled Germany, Holland, Spain, and, in excess, London, Nicola assisted to bring order into the room. Gazing at the dwindling array still awaiting attention, she enquired:

'Did you enjoy it, Candace? Travelling to all these places, I mean?'

Only too happy to abandon the dull chore of wrapping up and packing away what she had so joyously unwrapped, Candace watched Nicola neatly enveloping a Venetian Gondola in its mass of tissue paper.

'Yes,' but she spoke consideringly. 'Yes, I expect I did. But all of it didn't fascinate me, as it seemed to the others. We stayed in lovely hotels, and I admit it was a thrill to dress and dine in splendid surroundings. And I was excited to actually see monuments and places I'd read about in books—but everything wasn't all peaches and cream. I expect it was Drew's bringing-up that made me look on both sides of everything. Unexpectedly, Candace's serious mood vanished and she burst into an irrepressible chuckle.

'You should have seen Drew coaching me when I started my senior year in high school, and I began to get invitations for parties and dates. He didn't just tell me how to behave, he acted it with me. He used to say he knew how the pursuing was done, but I would be on the receiving end, and I'd better know the finer points of the game.

'You know, Nicola,' a reminiscent smile touched those still childish lips, 'I was told once how improper it was that a well brought up girl such as I purported to be should know as much as I did. It was just as well, however, that I did with that particular young gentleman. Drew. . . . He was right then as he always has been as far as I'm concerned. I'm so lucky to have him . . . I love him so much. I couldn't do anything he wouldn't approve of, but there's no other job I feel I could spend my life at.

'Oh, come on,' she exclaimed abruptly, 'let's dump the rest of this mess!' and grabbing the remains of her trip's garnerings she deposited them higgledy-piggledy into the open maw of a large suitcase. 'Drew told me you'd had a busy day, and I've just realised how selfish

I'm being, thinking only of myself. You have to work tomorrow too, sleep well!'

Nicola was thrust through Candace's door into her own. She closed it, flicked out the light, and climbed into bed, hoping that tiredness would indeed send her off to sleep without thinking.

CHAPTER NINE

HEAT, scorching the atmosphere, awaited their moving into the next morning, and it looked as if it was also going to be one of those days. The trip to the famous Coloured Sands of Teewah, instead of running smoothly as did most things Peter organised, got off to a bad start.

Viewed as a rising sun sent its shafts of light to bombard them, they were at their best in the early morning, but today a dozen things delayed the departure. Finally the loaded coach moved off, and more than Nicola heaved a sigh of relief.

They didn't often get such a disagreeable guest as the one who was responsible for most of the unpleasantness this morning. They got a lot like dear old Mr Fenton, who smiled at her now as he passed through the lobby. He was a sick man, but he loved fishing, and was only allowed on this fishing holiday because his doctor had decided to come too. He was the kindest, the gentlest person she had known, and made everyone happier for his presence.

They all watched out for him, endeavouring to see he didn't over-exert himself, and Jim would take him down to the beach in the Rover.

Well, Nicola thought, as she returned to her own province, that's that, they've gone at last. She ate lunch with Peter, then told him, 'I'm going to have a rest for a few hours. Nothing should come up, but nearly everyone is going fishing for tailor tonight, and I'd better be on deck in case I'm needed.'

Later, leaving the dinner table as she finished her meal, she shook her head reprovingly at Candace's and Gerry's behaviour. They were vying hilariously to see who could provide the most scandalous anecdote of their journeys abroad. She slipped up to her quarters to discard the Golden Citrus uniform for a straight skirt and cotton blouse, kicking off her shoes in exchange for soft towelling scuffs. With the big fish being brought in and being displayed for admiration, anyone could get in the way, and she wanted no saltwater stains or fish smells on her working gear.

Back at her desk, she tackled a stack of paper work and accounts to go out in the morning, left from the last two busy days. She merely laughed, and flipped a hand at invitations to go for the nightly perambulation on the beach, and finishing the pile of cardboard folders, knocked them on the desk top to straighten them before putting the lot tidily away in the drawer. She leaned on an elbow then, waiting for Peter, gazing out through the entrance and dreaming.

'Miss Grant ... Miss Grant!' The sound of her name being called in that breathless hurrying voice brought her swinging round. Mrs Hill was there beside her desk, supporting Mr Fenton, who was making an effort to draw away and stand upright. He tried to smile at Nicola, even if it was only a travesty of his usual greeting. She hurried out from behind her barricade; she had no need to ask what was the matter. Mrs Hill was already informing her of that in a distressed voice.

'It's one of his attacks. I'll get him to his room if I'm able. I've given him his tablets, but would you run down to the beach? Doctor Gault is fishing only a little way up ... towards Noosa, not the Coloured Sands way. Tell him about this.' She murmured more softly in an aside, 'Be as quick as you can, dear, won't you?'

Needing no second bidding, remembering that ashen face trying so hard to smile reassuringly at her, Nicola was out the door and running for the guarding dunes, taking the ramp at a much too fast a pace. She passed three fishermen before coming to Doctor Gault. He wasted no time asking useless questions, for when she stammered the name of Mr Fenton, he shoved his rod into her hand. 'Here, hold this,' he told her. 'Just hold it. Don't try to wind it in—I'll send someone along to do that.'

Nicola held on to the rod for dear life. It seemed to her unaccustomed grip to weigh a ton. The wind was strong, buffeting her, and the waves were washing about her knees. Her hair was a tangled mass over her face and had to remain that way, as she clung tightly with both hands.

Suddenly, from out of the night, other hands were above hers and a calm voice said with a laugh in it, 'You can let go now. Fishing rods don't really have to be gripped as if they're your lifeline to eternity!'

Nicola didn't care how she was holding it as long as it was safe. She had come to realise down here how attached fishermen were to their own rods. So, relinquishing it thankfully, she flew back across the sand and up the ramp. No one was in the office, so she made her way to Mr Fenton's unit, squeezing through the half open door as she heard Mrs Hill and the doctor inside.

Another figure was also standing somewhat awkwardly by the back wall as if wishing himself far away. Gerry's unit was next door to Mr Fenton's, and Doctor Gault would not have said please or thank you when grabbing anyone he needed for assistance.

Nicola raised an enquiring eyebrow to him, but his reaction was merely a shrug and two outspread expressive hands. Then Doctor Gault was turning from the bed and his tone when he spoke was cheerful. 'There, that's that. He'll do nicely now.' He glanced round and smiled at both Gerry and Nicola. 'How's my rod?' he asked the latter.

'It's in good hands, I think. But I only heard a voice and felt the hands, but both the voice and the hands seemed quite competent, so I imagine it's safe, don't you?' She grinned back at him. 'Now, is there anything I can help with here?'

'No, everything is under control,' he told her, and held the door for her to pass out.

'Come and have a drink with me,' Gerry suggested, as he too made good his escape. 'You probably need it after all this!'

'Oh, no, Gerry. Just look at me! I'm in no state to go drinking,' she answered him. 'Also, to tell you the truth, I've had enough excitement for one evening.'

Waving goodnight and turning to go, she came face to face with Drew. He stopped his quickly moving strides abruptly, stiffly. He glanced from her to the closing door of the unit which still showed Gerry Redfern's figure silhouetted against the light before the door shut. His gaze travelled from her tangled untidy hair, to the bare expanse of skin she was trying unsuccessfully to cover and on to her bare feet ... again. Following the direction of that look, she remembered that she had kicked off her scuffs at the bottom of the ramp when she was flying for Doctor Gault; they were probably still there.

'Well, my cool and remote ice maiden, you're certainly out of character tonight!' Trying desperately to push a wet bedraggled shirt into a just as sodden waistband without much success, she heard the words come, soft, silken, and had cause to remember that tone from

another time. Her arm was roughly caught up and
she was swung round the side of the building, and a
new timbre in new words caused an alarmed gasp to
escape her.

'Now what ... what in the hell are you doing in this
condition, at this time of night, and in Redfern's unit?'

She was frightened, literally, at his held-in violence,
then anger came to her rescue at the insinuation the
words, and yes, the tone, carried. She tried to wrench
herself free and found she was pulled even closer,
utterly unable to move at all.

'You must be mad, the way you're speaking!' she
ejaculated, staring into that intense face merely inches
away. 'Or drunk?' she added.

Drew didn't reply to the accusation; he laughed. And
when he did speak, slurred and barely audible, the
sentence carried no reassurance.

'I'm not drunk, I only wish I were, and imagining
this scene. But yes, I think I must be mad, or at least
have been, to think about you as I've been doing—
a pre-permissive throwback, not to be touched or
handled carelessly. How stupid could I have been? But
if this is a free-for-all, and it certainly looks like it,
I might as well get in for my cut!'

The face wasn't inches away now—it came down
to blot out the lights and the buildings, the sky behind.
Then his lips were on hers, brutally savage, demanding,
claiming completely. His fingers moved, dragging the
loose shirt completely free. His hand, spread flat against
her bare back, pulled her even closer as it had once

before, fusing body to body. Then, with knowledge, the fingers moved a fraction—a hook sprang apart. Nicola's gasp was cut short against his lips and she felt his hand.... Clamped even closer, her whole torso mingled with his, she stood encircled, hating him in some remote recess of her mind, yet feeling his caresses send antagonism to the four winds, melting her metabolism, dispatching conscious thought flying.

A door was flung suddenly open, a lozenge of brilliance cut through to outline them—one unit with no separation at all. She was pushed back against the rough brick wall with an unexpectedness that left her stunned, and the sharply uttered expletive came back to her as Drew turned on his heel and left ... left her, abandoned, exhausted, leaning against the building at her back.

Straightening upright, slowly she made for her quarters. Back to the door, her hands fumbled blindly behind her and turned the key. Instinctively ... the action emanating from primitive times to make of this room a sanctuary. Crossing to the dressing table, she saw in the mirror some excuse for Drew's behaviour. Her hair was a tangled mess from the salt spray and wind, as she had stood in the ocean holding on for dear life to that rod put so suddenly in her charge. It did look as if she had slept in it. Her blouse, now completely out of her bedraggled skirt, showed a ribbon strap hanging loose about an elbow, and as she gazed at it, the face reflected took on a fiery tint as memory washed over her ... a hand went up to her eyes.

All in all, she shrugged resignedly, not a picture of her usual self. She also wondered, gazing at her bare feet, if she would ever see the gaily-coloured towelling scuffs again.

Tiredly she picked up her brush and, with less than her usual brisk strokes, her hair was returned to its normal smoothness. Along with her face, her lips lifted to the deluge of water the hot shower poured down upon them, but no amount of water could erase the memory of that scorching embrace of a few short minutes ago.

Slipping into a nightdress, she was turning down the bed when she heard footsteps outside on the path, and stepped swiftly across to flick out the light.

Candace's cool voice floated through the open transom. 'Thanks for the drink, Peter. I'm off to bed now. See you in the morning!'

Nicola heard Peter answer, then his footsteps receding. In bed, she lay wondering what to do. Her first decision of packing and catching Mr Torrens as he went past in the morning, she had discarded. There would be too much talk; too much wondering.... For the kind of job she intended to get, she wanted no idle gossip following her. Finally she decided to go to work as usual in the morning, give Peter a week's notice saying that she was going to Brisbane as she had originally planned, that she thought she needed a more industrialised atmosphere. She would also keep well out of Drew's way ... just wouldn't she! And then, as if her thoughts had conjured him up out of the darkness, footsteps sounded outside and Drew's voice called:

'Nicola!'

She lay rigid, silent. He knocked then, and his voice asked, 'Open the door, Nicola. I want to speak to you!'

Silent still, for she had no intention of opening any door, she decided how lucky she was that she had locked it.

'I know you're not asleep, Nicola,' he said again. 'I wish to see you, so you had better open this bloody door.'

Candace's door opened instead, and the silent girl in the next unit heard her say, 'For heaven's sake, Drew, what are you going on about? Nicola has probably gone to bed hours ago. If she hasn't, she doesn't want to see you, because no one could remain oblivious of your presence with the pandemonium you're cooking up!'

A new voice made itself heard and light reflected upon Nicola's ceiling, as a door further along was set ajar. 'What's all the racket? Isn't there supposed to be some rule or another that it's mandatory to be quiet around sleeping quarters? I want to be up early to catch the tide, and with all this hell of a row going on, how can I get my sleep?'

Drew's tone took on that slurred softness it always got when he was angry, and that he was angry there was no doubt. He answered, 'I'm sorry, but we've had an emergency with illness. There'll be no more noise, I promise you.'

'In that case, then ...' the peevish voice resumed, 'goodnight!' A door closed.

Two curt sentences were exchanged next door, then heavy footsteps departed. Nicola slid down on her pillows and pulled the light blanket folded across the bottom of the bed up about her. It was high summer and quite warm, but she felt chilled. And it was not until the quiet hours that preceded the dawn had also wended their way into the reaches of time that her heavy eyelids came to rest finally upon her cheeks.

However, she was at her desk at the usual hour, well groomed, welcoming, her normal cool smile in evidence. Though there might be dark shadows beneath her eyes, her attention to detail was as meticulous as it had always been.

Drew had been already in Reception when she put in her appearance, and she thanked heaven she had more than one guest clamouring for her attention. He remained at the entrance door, gazing out over the ocean, his intention plain to her. He came across at last, and after a swift glance at his expression she glanced just as swiftly away. He told her curtly:

'You might have told me the reason you were at Redfern's unit, Nicola. No one likes to realise they've made a fool of themselves!'

Not looking at him, she answered flatly, 'You gave me no chance to tell you anything.'

Not even the faintest tinge of pink coloured her cheeks as her reply came. They were as pale as a normally tanned skin could be. 'And,' she continued, 'I have no intention of telling you anything today, either. I was going to see Peter after breakfast to give him my notice, but you'll do just as well. I would like to leave in a week, please—or sooner, if you can get some-one up from the city before then.'

A hand, tanned almost to black, dropped over the fingers restlessly pushing papers into neat piles. His grip was cruel, merciless, and his voice, silken, decep-tively gentle, was barely audible.

'You'd better be on the cliff-top after breakfast, because if you're not, I'm coming here to get you—or to your quarters. And I don't give a damn whom it disturbs, or how much commotion it causes, my dear Miss Grant. So think of that over your meal and know that I mean what I say.'

Her fingers were released and she gazed down at them, all squashed together with the deeply indented marks of his grip still upon her wrist.

Jim, coming to stand beside her, broke the trance in which she was held. He was dangling a pair of scuffs before her. Gazing at them, she began to laugh, but quickly put up a hand to stop herself. Hysterics would get her nowhere.

'These look like yours, Miss Grant,' Jim was saying. 'I expect you kicked them off when you ran for the doctor last night,' and he leaned over and dropped them behind her counter.

CHAPTER TEN

IN the event, Nicola didn't have to decide if she would go out to the cliff-top. They ate their breakfast, Drew silent, his brow a thundercloud, Gerry trying outrageously to make time with Candace, who, while quite willing to meet him half-way, was thinking only of getting to Brisbane—and a hospital. She would see him there, she grinned up at him, knowing that this was his last day here.

Peter, of course, wouldn't notice an emotionally charged atmosphere if he fell over it; it would simply have no part in his existence. He got on with the business of shovelling in fuel, then departed, muttering about checking that damned trip. Nicola just sat drinking her fruit juice; a cup of tea, and crumbling the toast on her plate. Then, unexpectedly, Peter was back.

'Hi there, Nicola,' he greeted her, grinning delightedly. 'You've never actually been to the Coloured Sands, have you? It just hasn't been convenient somehow. But two of the party on the trip this morning have pulled out, so I thought that as Candace will be leaving almost immediately, you and she could go in their place. How about it?'

'Oh, good!' Candace, all for fun and tripping around, smiled. 'I really can't go back to Brisbane without seeing them, and it will save you taking me, Drew. So come on, Nicola, hurry up!'

Nicola didn't look at Drew. She glanced up at Peter. 'Can you manage the desk while it's busy at this hour, Peter? I'd like to go. I might not get the chance again.'

Peter's astonished, 'I just told you to go, didn't I?' contrasted with Drew's soft, cold, 'Oh, I think there's no chance, none at all, of your not ever seeing them,' as he pushed back his chair with a jerk that sent it spinning across the floor.

Nicola also pushed back her chair, to set it neatly beneath the table. Hurrying after Candace, she walked beside her to their quarters. There, quickly slipping out of her uniform but shying away from donning a skirt and blouse, she quickly pulled on jeans and an over-blouse, then slipped on a knitted band around her hair to keep it from flying all over the place—she wanted no reminder of the way it had appeared last night.

The two girls walked out to the big lorry-cum-coach and were helped up the high steps. Canopied above, the sides were open, and as they sped along, swiftly flying, the creaming tumbled waves, the hard-packed sand and silver dunes, swung together, until they were a part of the vividness imparted by a golden day and the indigo blue of seas and sky.

Nicola might not be able to forget Drew, but she

could push the memory of him away while this exhilarating drive was in progress. It was like rushing
through space itself. Only the low sand-dunes were to
the left of them; in front was mile after uncounted mile
of wide, empty beach, with the blue restless ocean
stretching to the very edge of the world guarding their
right. The vast arch above was so deep, so vivid, that
she felt she could reach out and gather armfuls of
colour.

A first sign of the Sands appearing in a jagged de-
sign upon the cliff face filled her with a faint disappointment. It looked quite attractive with the early
morning sun striking upon it, but surely.... Then from
the top of cliffs, rising higher above the silver sand
came shapes and formations, their colours beginning
from pale sandstone to violent yellow and glaring
ochre. Here and there, as if nature was not wanting to
be too prodigal with sheer beauty, a dash of crimson
red shading to orange made its appearance. And, even
more sparsely yet, the glow of purple, deep and eyecatching, caused the whole busload to turn for yet
another look.

'Are you coming nearer to see them close up,
Nicola?' Candace called, as they dropped down to
stand among the other tourists.

'No, I don't think so, but you go, Candace. I'm just
going to sit here and stare.' She sat upon the yielding
soft sand, as the others moved away, laughing, talking,
or just doing their own thing. She didn't think, just
was, allowing the warmth and colour of her surround-

ings to soothe and bring their own style of comfort.

Driving back in a happier frame of mind brought her to actually think of last night, instead of pushing it as far back in her consciousness as she was able to. Whatever the evidence, Drew shouldn't have thought, never mind act, as he had done, she decided, and wondered suddenly where she would be this time next Saturday. Well, you played the cards as they fell. She shrugged, and gave herself up to their swiftly moving progress.

'Oh, thank God you're home, Nicola!' Peter called to her, before she had time to get inside when the coach cruised to the entrance of the resort. 'Look, come and help me juggle some bookings around—if you can. We've just had a phone call for accommodation for ten extra guests. I can't see, however,' he added ruefully, 'how we're to fit them in. But I certainly don't intend to turn them away as Drew told me to do. I can't understand him lately. It's his business, this place, and it's his damned money too, and he's acting as if he couldn't care less!'

Not replying to this last sentence, Nicola merely said, 'Give me a minute to change, Peter, then we'll see what can be done.'

And something had been done when the bus arrived with the extra visitors. Bookings had been juggled, but even so, they couldn't be stretched like elastic, and it was with some trepidation that she had finally suggested:

'If Drew wouldn't mind having you and Gerry (he

wouldn't mind as he goes home anyway tomorrow, in the pre-breakfast lift), Peter, in a double bunk in his sitting room for just one night, we could work it. Candace could move in with me, then, with those double vacancies....'

Peter was jubilant, but Nicola wondered what Drew would say about having his privacy invaded—if he allowed it to be.

The resort manager had no such reservations. 'It's not something I would propose as a general rule,' he explained. 'But Gerry is beginning to be such a friend of Candace's that he's almost one of the family. And Drew can damn well put up with me in his sitting room for one night. We're just starting out and we need any and every advertisement that comes our way. Also, we're lucky that it's the Gala tonight. They should like that.' He caught sight of her expression. 'Good heavens,' he ejaculated, 'don't tell me you'd forgotten!'

Of course she had forgotten. Last night had made normal, ordinary happenings slide completely from her mind.

There had been some big tailor caught, and when an agent had rung for a coachload booking for dinner only, Peter had decided to combine the two occasions, and came up with the idea of a Gala dinner. It would be a brilliantly moonlit night, and as their restaurant was beginning to be talked about as a different and romantic out-of-the-way place to dine, he had declared he would make it a night to be remembered.

A pencil in her mouth, chewing at its top as she concentrated, Nicola finally surveyed the scored and rescored reservation list, saying a trifle diffidently, 'There it is, then. I'll make out a clean sheet so we'll actually be able to read it without thinking it's written in code. You will see Drew and get his permission first, though, won't you?' This last sentence she asked quite anxiously. She received a nod in return, and an, 'Okay, don't panic, I will. He's over at the homestead now, but I'll see him as soon as he comes back.'

She was thankful that all the manipulating this unexpected influx entailed meant that she wouldn't have to see Drew at lunch time. She and Candace helped the girls set up extra beds, and finally, after checking that everything that could be prepared had been done, they had both eaten a scratch meal, self-provided, in the staff dining-room.

Candace glanced at her companion with a rueful grin, exclaiming, 'What a hell of a mess we've made of your room! Do you think we'll ever get it into some sort of order?'

Remembering how they had left the unit after dumping Candace's possessions helter-skelter into it, Nicola could only give her shoulders a shrug, saying indifferently, 'What does it matter, we can always walk over things.'

Passing the dining-room entrance later, she stopped. 'Who did those cut-outs?' she asked. One whole side of the large room was a frieze of palm trees. Not paintings; the trees could be growing there with cunningly placed lights serving to heighten that impression.

'The boss,' was Jim's laconic answer.

She wondered if it were Peter or Drew Jim had in mind. And, on a step-ladder reaching high to tie a string of amazingly large, gaily-coloured balloons that swept across the ceiling like a sunburst, Jim answered her unasked question as he stepped on to the floor again.

'Mr Huntly. Good, aren't they? You can almost believe you're up in the north, where the palms really rustle in an ocean breeze.'

'Yes, they certainly give that impression,' but Nicola was answering absently. She was gazing intently at the frieze. It gave to the whole room a sense of the exotic, of what Pacific islands were all about. And of course, Drew would be able to do this sort of thing. He was an architect, after all, used to drawing and creating designs. She gave a last glance around; at the shining glasses and silver-ware; the gay coloured hibiscus floating in bowls on every table, the glowing citrus gold of the linen; at all the embellishments for this gala dinner tonight . . . and was satisfied. She might be finished with the resort, but her professional pride still took pleasure in excellence. For Peter's sake she wanted the guests to enjoy and remember this coming night.

'Look, Peter,' she said, finding him checking the bar supplies, 'I'm off for a while. All accounts and papers are as finalised as they can be. I'm going up to the unit before it's time to dress. It's been a hectic last night and today, and I don't want to end up with a headache.'

A headache was something she seldom suffered, but it covered as an excuse for a multitude of sins.

That swung him round from his muttering about whisky and vodka to really look at her. 'Hell, Nicola, am I really working you too hard? Yes, go and see if you can snatch a couple of hours. As you said, where your department is concerned, all is in readiness. Even tonight, there's not a great deal for you to do. Only you must be on tap. I need your know-how if anything goes wrong.

'Go on,' he added, 'try and fit in a little nap, then bathe and slip into something really glamorous. After all, that's what tonight's all about—a glamorous way to spend an evening. So remember, we'll all have to live up to it. Off you go, sweetie!' He gave her a pat on the bottom, sending her on her way for all the world like a doting uncle to a particularly loved five-year-old.

Nicola did depart, walking the familiar way to her quarters without even seeing it. Once there among the chaos, thankful that Candace had gone off somewhere, she undressed, slipping into a soft, loose dressing gown. Lying down on her bed, she bunched the pillow behind her head. But as her eyes closed they flew abruptly open again. Drew's image had settled directly before them.

Why on earth had they started off—and continued— as they had? His attitude had antagonised her on the night he had come to her father's shack—though she admitted she had reacted badly, because given his due, he had done only what he considered right.

She hadn't taken other men in instant dislike as she had seemed to do with him; and she had had invitations in plenty from them up north, and accepted some. She had known how to handle them as well, Gerry being a case in point. For some of these assignations she had dressed and gone wondering what the night would bring. Of course she had hoped to find romance, and a man to love—didn't every girl, in spite of all this new liberation?

Well, she had found it with a vengeance now: and much good it had done her. Supine, she lay there, wondering.

'Oh dear! I'd forgotten.' Candace had tripped over a gaping suitcase as she opened the door to step inside. The light snapped on, bringing brilliance to a shadowy room. Nicola smiled across at her. Not only because she was Drew's sister, either. Candace could have been so different a person, allowing for what she had and was.

'I'll get my shower first, Candace, if you don't mind,' Nicola said, swinging her legs off the bed to stand upright.

'Be my guest. I've still got to go through this mess to find something to wear.' A hand went out in a throwaway gesture to the shambles surrounding them. 'Anyway, what does one wear to a gala in the wilds of Australia?'

'I should imagine,' firmness now coloured Nicola's

words: her decision as to what she herself would be wearing. If she was leaving, she would leave with all flags flying. 'I should imagine,' she repeated dryly, 'much like what you would wear to a gala on the Mediterranean coast—given that it wasn't a grand ball. After all, to pay our prices, our guests must own more than the odd penny.'

In the shower, she reached out, flipping on taps, then carefully protecting her hair as a gesture to the coming evening, stepped under the streaming water as hot as she could stand it. As she stood with face lifted to it, some of the tension was washed from her. Adjusting the taps, she turned them from hot, gasping as the needle-points of coldness poured upon her.

'It's all yours, Candace,' she told the other girl, still rummaging among her scattered possessions. Deliberately, she slipped into scanty underclothes, and as deliberately sat at the dressing table to begin on her make-up. Blue-green eye-shadow went on with a more than lavish hand, lipstick with a heavier pressure. She was pulling the model dress over her brushed shining hair as Candace returned.

'Here, I'll help you.' Candace took hold of the zip from reaching fingers and slid it shut. As she ran her glance over the girl standing so close, an eyebrow went up—goodness, she was like Drew now!—as she drawled, 'Doing it up a bit brown, aren't you, Nicola? Or are you imagining this *is* Monte Carlo? I'd better get busy now too, to try and match that. Then we'll go out and knock 'em cold, shall we?'

'It's not too bare?' For her life's sake, Nicola couldn't keep the tinge of anxiety from her tone.

'Well, it all depends.' Laughter echoed in the reply. 'If you don't want people ... men ... to turn for a second look, I'd say it was too bare. On the other hand.... Oh, come on, Nicola, don't be silly. You look lovely. And, I may add, so does that dress. We'll go and see how Peter's first gala is shaping up. You'd think he was having a real baby, the way he's carrying on!'

Behind her desk, as she had explained to Peter earlier, Nicola was the only one in the whole complex who was not busy. Squeezing time out for it, Peter brought to her a large topless pineapple—a real one, she saw, taking hold of it. He grinned as she gazed dubiously at the two drinking straws.

'This one's innocuous, I promise you. But I thought you'd like to try one of our specials. Because we need you on deck,' he laughed gaily across at her, teeth flashing, happy, 'I told them to omit its sudden death ingredient. Enjoy it, love. You too must have sparkle tonight. Drink to success!'

Nicola took an experimental sip from the pineapple shell just as Candace came wandering through to Reception, carrying an identical concoction in her hand. They leaned against the barricade, one inside, one out, in companionable silence as they drank. Finishing what Peter had christened 'the Teewah Cocktail', Candace placed her container on top of the counter.

'Go and have a look-see at all the fun and games,

Nicola,' she said. 'I'll keep an eye on the desk for you.'

Gazing at her a little doubtfully, Nicola grinned, saying, 'Okay, I'll go see how the other half lives.' She made her way through the dining-room, past the glowing Namatjira, and stood in the archway leading through to the lounge.

The tables were packed, and, it seemed from the amount of noise and laughter issuing forth, the gala was going with a bang. Balloons were being reached for far above, beautiful, many-coloured, floating. Both Drew and the barman were behind the bar, she noticed, seeing him for the first time since this morning. Peter was circulating, and the four girls were juggling trays. Even Mrs Hill was helping.

Nicola smiled to herself, happy for Peter. This was his baby—this gala dinner. Instead of returning to the desk, she wandered outside. Gazing along the terrace which fronted the whole complex, she saw that here too, most of the small tables were occupied. She was hailed from one of these, then saw that the two men at it were dining, not merely drinking.

'Why, Mr Jenkins,' she smiled at the big genial guest who had accosted her, 'not going inside for dinner tonight?'

'No fear! I'm not falling for that caper. It's bad enough at home when the wife makes me. Imagine being in there with that mob!' he threw out a derogatory arm in the direction of the sound-filled rooms behind. 'No, a bloke would be mad to be in there when he could be down on the beach, fishing for the big

ones. I will say this, though,' he added in a different
tone, 'that young Sinclair has done us proud, even if
we didn't dine inside.' Contentedly he rubbed where
his meal had disappeared to. Nicola laughed, wished
them good fishing and returned to Reception.

CHAPTER ELEVEN

'I NEED an extra pair of hands to help me, so, Candace, you're nominated.' Peter came hurrying to grab
hold of Candace to propel her before him. 'I do realise
bubbly needs the expert touch,' he laughed down at
her, 'but you have a pair of hands for carrying.'

Nicola caught at his arm as he made to move swiftly
away. 'Look, is there something I can make myself
busy with, Peter? Everyone else is occupied, and no
one needs the desk at this time of night.'

Peter stopped his rush for a brief moment. 'You'd
be more hindrance than help serving dinner, I expect,
but the bar is in a hell of a shambles. Ask Drew if you
can give a hand there.'

Nicola had no intention of asking Drew anything, so,
of her own accord, she drifted through on to the terrace.
She began to collect used glasses, the remains of crisps
and nuts in their soiled empty dishes, wiping the tables

as she cleared them. She took a tray of dirty glasses inside and set it on the bar in front of Jim, who was washing them, then reached for another tray. Turning, she saw who was looking at her, a question asked by an eyebrow raised higher than any eyebrow had a right to be.

'I'm helping to get the terrace tables cleared,' she felt impelled to explain. 'Everyone else is run off their feet, and I'm not needed in Reception—at least, not yet.'

'Certainly, do that. Feel free to help. You'll be doing it for some time yet, you know.'

She stared back into those inimical grey-black eyes, her own wanting to express just as much determination. She turned on her heel and left.

She let the cool soothing ocean breeze blow over her, as she brought cleanliness and order on to the terrace once again, and listened absently to the lilting dinner music. Sitting at the piano, the player was drifting through ballads, softly, weaving a web of enchantment in which to enjoy the art of eating. Later, no doubt, Nicola expected, he would be joined by other musicians engaged for the dancing.

She glanced at her watch, and returning inside found Candace searching for her. 'Come on, Nicola, I've been looking for you. The chef is just bringing in the highlight of the evening. Oh!' The lights of the whole front of the complex went dark, only moonlight providing any illumination at all. Candace's grip on her arm tightened, and Nicola saw the tall white figure with his taller chef's cap standing high enter through the darkened kitchen doorway. Vivid blue flames cast their flaring shadows as the Bombe Alaska was carried proudly outstretched in both hands.

He was followed by a second white-clad figure, then a third. Glynis, also wearing an overall and a tall white hat, marched behind the two men, their flaming burdens sending phantoms dancing with flickering blue fire.

Candace, those grey eyes, so like her brother's, glowing, her smile wide, asked, as the lights made their reappearance, 'There, wasn't that just something? That's Peter for you! It's that little extra touch which makes all the difference. I only hope he makes sure, however, there's some left for us.' She gave a surreptitious glance at her watch and continued, 'And if this mob doesn't hurry up and finish, it will be midnight before we sample it. And at midnight I have a surprise I want to produce—or at least, Peter and I have.'

Nicola cast a swift sideways glance, and was instantly reassured. There was nothing between Peter and Candace. Both of them, the elder girl reflected, were single-minded about their careers. She did wonder fleetingly, however, why Elspeth wasn't here for the gala.

All attention on the serving of Bombe Alaska, no one noticed Jim reach up and give a jerk, but suddenly, all over the room, large globes of colour, red and blue, green and yellow, crimson and purple, came floating down. They were soon scooped up by eager fingers, and Nicola thought suddenly—balloons! Such simple things to provide that air of delight and gaiety. Peter's first big night was certainly going to be an unqualified success.

He came towards them now, grinning down at the two girls in the doorway, his expression contented, smug.

'Hungry?' he asked. 'I realise it's just a trifle past our regular dinner hour. . . .'

'Oh, just a trifle,' interjected Candace, mimicking him, 'but don't let it worry you. We'll be imitating Spanish dining time—going on for eleven. I only hope the chef has saved something for us to make up for it!'

Finishing his own discourse, taking no notice of her acid comments, Peter continued, 'Glynis will have our table ready in a few ticks. Bide your soul . . . or another part of your anatomy . . . in patience. Oh, just a second, I'm needed. . . .' He was off.

Their table ready for them at last, they ate accompanied by the dance music coming to them from out of the lounge, and, if there was constraint between two of their party, the rest seemed not to notice. Getting her wish, Candace dived into the Bombe Alaska which had indeed been saved for them. Then, unexpectedly, Peter was pouring a bubbling, sparkling liquid into hollow-stemmed glasses beside each plate. Catching sight of the label, Nicola raised an eyebrow at Peter, saying softly:

'Bunging it on a bit, aren't you?' She handled the accounts and the costing invoices!

He didn't answer immediately, just passed on to pour his own drink, before glancing around the other four at the table, and then at his watch. He said, 'It's just on midnight. Happy birthday, Nicola. May it always be as happy as tonight has been.'

Raising her glass as well, Candace grinned delightedly, then getting into the act came Gerry. 'But of course, even though I'd no idea. Happy birthday, Nicola. May there be many more of them.'

Unable to prevent herself, Nicola slid a glance at the figure sitting opposite and met frowning grey eyes. The gaze shifted, went the rounds of the table; his voice, unamused, added, 'It seems I'm the last to be informed of pending events. Still,' he raised his glass as the others had done, 'happy birthday, Nicola.'

At his words, the colour flamed in her face and she gazed accusingly at Candace. 'I didn't tell anyone my birthday date. How did you know?'

'Do you remember, Nicola?' the younger girl laughed. 'You said you didn't believe that rubbish, when I was reading out loud what the stars forecast the other day. I asked when you were born. Checking out a busload of fishermen, you probably didn't take in what I was talking about. But I remembered!' Candace was enjoying herself.

Holding the wine-glass between both hands before her face, she looked triumphantly out through the rising bubbles and said again to the girl sitting silently across from her, 'Happy birthday to you, dear Nicola. Especially for knowing some girls who've gone in for nursing.' She put the champagne to her lips.

Toasted, embarrassed a little, Nicola drank her imported champagne too, and it was Peter who broke it up. He drained his glass, flipped his hand, then went about his duties, Drew following him.

Gerry thrust a hand through each of the girls' arms and walked them outside. They paused on the terrace, Gerry seeking a vacant table. Dropping into the chair held for her, thinking of the man who had just left so abruptly after Peter, Nicola gazed out over a moon-washed sea of sparkling beaten silver—a diamond-painted mirror, edged with a creaming froth of lace.

Gerry returned, bringing them both a tall glass of pineapple with lots of crushed ice, and they sat idly sipping until the music resumed, when Gerry took Candace in to dance.

Nicola walked down the ramp and from there on to the beach. She kept to the fine soft sand and strolled slowly along, thinking of the scene Candace had just precipitated, and thinking too that she was now indeed twenty years of age. A milestone! Well, she shrugged, saying to herself, 'Brisbane, here I come, I hope we get to like each other ... we'd better, as far as I'm concerned, anyway.' She turned then, with a second shrug, and made her way back to the ramp, giving one last long look at the silver wash spreading to the end of the world, then ran quickly from log to log up the incline. She stepped on to the cliff-top, almost bumping into the man who waited there.

Her arm was caught before she could move away, and Drew's words came bleakly. 'I'll walk you up to the lounge. The gala is finishing in ten minutes, so you might as well be there.'

She went, because she was forced to. The musicians were swinging into the last dance of the night, and Drew's arms were about her, tightly, unable to be cast aside. Perforce she danced, as he held her closely. The music changed, but the arm about her gripped still, as they stood for the National Anthem.

Jim was dismantling the umbrellas; the girls were clearing away. With no option, her elbow still in Drew's fingers, Nicola walked beside him as he moved towards the kitchen. Guessing he was taking a short cut through the back way, she wondered at him using the little corridor between the storerooms and kitchen, but pride would not allow her to ask anything of him. The door of the baggage chamber was flung open, and with a flick of the finger came a dim light from above. A shoulder thrust against the door and the world was shut out.

He turned then, a hand coming to rest on either side of the wall behind, her body held prisoner within. 'There'll be people roaming round for hours yet,' the low silken voice came down to her, 'if I know the signs after such a night as this has been. So it's no use walking you up to your unit, even if Candace wasn't sharing it, and I tell you, Nicola, I've put up with enough interruptions and evasions today to strain to the full any patience I have left.

'Now, why didn't you tell me last night that it was Fenton's room you were in, and for what reason?' He waited her out, so she answered curtly.

'You didn't give me much chance. Also, I'll have you know, my friends ... the men I know ... wouldn't go jumping to the conclusions that you seem to have done. I don't feel very flattered by them!'

She felt the arms hemming her in go even more rigid. 'If you could only have seen yourself,' the words were uttered in the man's slowest drawl, tight with what she supposed was anger. 'If only you could have seen yourself,' he repeated even more softly. 'I was thinking of you when I saw you ... saw you looking as you did, emerging from Redfern's unit. You think you were manhandled ... God, you don't realise how lucky you were that that light blazed across us when it did. I can tell you, I had quite different intentions ... and they had no place in them for allowing you to rush off on your own.

'Furious, more angry than I'd ever been, making my way to the beach to try to walk it off—I ran into Peter going to check on Fenton, and learned the story of the night.

'Then, of course, you wouldn't answer my knock. By this time I couldn't have cared if the whole resort had gone up in flames. But between that fellow complaining about noise, and Candace ticking me off, I decided it would be better not trying to break down your raking door.'

The figure looming above her was so close. She knew what was about to happen ... she wanted his lovemaking, but.... She turned restlessly. Nothing had gone right where they were involved, and where Drew was concerned her will-power disintegrated with his first caress. Restlessly she twisted again between those imprisoning arms. It was no use. An arm left the wall at her side and went behind her back. His hand spread hard, flatly against it. But beneath those fingers there was no bare skin this time. It made no difference. She was drawn against him, her entire body along his, length to length. She was not kissed, however, but she felt the tenseness of his muscles communicate to her senses.

'God, Nicola,' he muttered, his lips resting beside her throat, 'I've had enough of this on-again, off-again caper. I'm not cut out for it. I want to take you back to your unit. I want to stay with you....' From its resting place, his mouth shifted, settling at last on the lips lifted to meet it. It was different this time—giving and taking, not just accepting this scorching tide of passion that flared between them.

It lasted a moment, or an hour ... she only knew she didn't want it to finish. Her senses weren't flying off leaving her unaware, either; she knew she was here, she knew she was with Drew. She wanted everything he wanted. Totally against him, the hand at her back unable to bring her closer, she melted into his caresses.

It could have been almost a groan that recalled her to their surroundings. Abruptly, she was not lying against him—she was being stood away with both hands at her waist.

'Hell and damnation!' Utterly unlike any of the tones she had become accustomed to in Drew's voice, the expletive came, tense, strained. 'Look, I could go on, and I think you wouldn't stop me. But tomorrow would come, bringing its own regrets of hasty decisions. Also I've got some unfinished business of my own to attend to.'

Elspeth? she thought. And, by her attitude, Elspeth certainly showed she had squatter's rights. Had she? The atmosphere was too charged with emotion, and a cold breath seemed to come between them, but Drew was turning her towards the door, speaking still in that strained timbre as he flicked out the light. 'Come on, we'll get out of here while we still have some sense left.'

They stood a moment in the dimly-lit corridor, but Nicola's entire being was still in that small room behind them. Dazedly, she remembered when she had last stood in this hallway. It couldn't have been more different, crowded with fishermen standing where she and Drew now stood. They had been facing the hatchway into the kitchen and watched intently as their own particular fish, tagged with its plastic disc, was expertly filleted and put to grill lightly with butter—or steeped in egg and breadcrumbs, to be turned out crisp and golden brown, from its deep oil fry.

Then, triumphantly carrying their harvest from the sea with their own fair hands, they marched into the dining room. No waitress was important enough to carry *this* burden.

Nicola shook her head, sending the hazy vision of other days flying. There were no laughing fishermen's voices echoing in the narrow corridor now, and with her hand warm in Drew's, she walked sedately from this place by his side.

Under the overhang of the unit that Candace was sharing with her for the night, her escort reached out and turned the handle, leaving the door slightly ajar. He pulled her close, enfolding her completely, his heart, heavy, thudding, pounding against her.

'Look, my love,' he said abruptly, his hands about her waist, standing her away, 'I don't want to part with you so soon, but to stay would inevitably lead to the point of no return. So what do you say to a burn along the beach? The breeze could blow some common sense into us, and it's such a night as you, being you, would find romantic. Silver moonlight, low-hanging stars, murmuring waves. . . .' His voice, even though still husky with emotion, held the tinge of laughter in its depth.

'Oh, yes! Oh, yes, Drew. Thank you for thinking of it.' She made to raise herself for his kiss, but the clasping hands stayed her.

'No, you don't! This drive is for therapeutic reasons—to blow a wind of coolness through us both, and bring us home pleasantly tired ... I hope. So you bear that in mind even if I don't manage to.'

'Anything you say.' And tonight, Nicola knew, it would be anything he said. 'But I can't go in this,' her hand indicated her dress.

'I should think not! If I told the truth, that give-away neck line was the reason for all my interest. Didn't you know?' A laugh still lingered in his voice as he continued, 'Go and change. I'll go get the Land Rover keys. They're one thing I don't keep in my dress pants pockets. You've got five minutes.' He was gone.

It took less than that to throw off her lovely dress and slip into a cotton frock and some beach scuffs. She added, though, a touch of lipstick, even if it was going to be only moonlight, before tying a chiffon scarf around her hair.

In the direction of her midriff was that empty feeling again; the same sensation that was usually a pre-requisite upon entering a dentist's surgery. She knew the way she felt—even just to remember the way in which Drew had kissed her melted her very bones. But Drew ... he was a practised man of the world, experienced in all kinds of situations ... making love certainly one of them. What were his real intentions? What was it he had said about an 'on-again, off-again caper—that he was not cut out for'? However, he *had* said a moment ago. 'Come for a burn along the beach.' So she would see what a burn along the beach brought.

He was waiting for her, lounging against the front fender, gazing out over the ocean. He straightened when she made her appearance, but he had no smile for her and those grey eyes were hooded. But flying along what was becoming familiar territory by this time, the wind blowing her hair all over the place despite the scarf, he turned unexpectedly, his eyes wide, a smile altering his whole expression. Nicola caught her breath sharply. No one could smile in that manner at someone without meaning. . . . She leaned closer to her window, allowing the cool ocean breeze to blow upon hot cheeks. Abruptly, the Rover was pulled to a sliding halt, emptiness around it as far as the eye could see. To the north where the beach stretched to infinity; to the south towards Noosa and the lights of civilisation—with the moon-washed, diamond-sparkled water on one side, and the high dunes which were just beginning to merge into the Coloured Sands on the other.

Drew jumped down, passed around the bonnet to swing open her door. He lifted up both hands and Nicola slid down into the arms waiting to enfold her. She was clamped tight, and as his head came down, her arms rose automatically to clasp behind his neck.

It was a long, long time before that head came upright again, and even then she was not released, only set back against the metal of the fender within the close grip of his arms. One hand let the back of his fingers trail across her cheek to rest just above the low neck of her dress. His voice, low and teasing, came from above her head.

'God! Doing this has been the only thought in my mind for weeks; the raking days seemed to stretch on for ever. Still, it was worth waiting for, my ice-maiden. Am I allowed to inform you that when you do thaw, you certainly do it with panache; throwing to the four winds any and all inhibitions with which you've kept me at arm's length for so long. I realise we didn't start out with the most promising of episodes, but why....'

'The night I was abducted and brought here, there was Elspeth,' her voice held more than a trace of breathlessness as she answered. 'And the way she behaved left no doubt—in fact, it gave every indication that she had more than just a casual claim on you—*that* can't be missed with that kind of involvement.'

'Elspeth? Yes, well..,; I hadn't met you then, and she is a dish, isn't she? But my unfinished business is finished.' The words held dismissal, and that was all she would be told about Elspeth, she knew.

She could feel the hand that lay so confidently against her breast, and the other hand at the small of her back, holding her against him—and she didn't care about Elspeth any longer. This was Drew, and she knew she would have to accept him exactly as he was.

His hands released her, slowly, as if with reluctance, and, taking her wrist, he walked her to the glittering mirror that was the water. There he stood suddenly still, laughter breaking out, full-bodied, amusement all through it.

'Peter's going to kill me,' he said. Her face turned, and he answered it. 'You don't think things are going to remain as they are, do you?'

'Oh, I didn't think.... What are ... what will we do?'

'I expect you can stay until he trains someone, but it will have to be a damn quick training.'

'Couldn't I live in your unit, my lord and master, while you commute?' Her words were only half joking; taking in the tone he had used a moment ago.

He grabbed her and swung her round. 'Bear those words in mind! I like them! And no, you're not staying in my unit. Where I am, there you're going to be too.' His tone lost the granite it had held, as he continued, 'Look, the tide is coming in,' he lifted her and swung her to safety from a further than usual breaking wave. 'It will be over the beach quite soon, and to have the Land Rover swamped would only add insult to injury as far as Peter is concerned, so I expect....' He took her hand and began running.

He laughed back over his shoulder at her and called, 'Come along, my love, I'll race you to our chariot!' They fled across the sand in the brilliant white moonlight, to where in the distance, standing stark and lonely in that vast empty expanse, the Land Rover waited to receive them.

Nicola didn't sit by the window on the way back. To be able to sit close to Drew naturally was a sensation she wasn't going to forgo. He looked away from the tunnel of light the headlamps were blazing as if trying to outvie the brilliance of the cascading moonlight, and smiled down at her. Such a smile, Nicola thought; so different.... Her heart went out to him and what she felt must have shown.

'Cut it out, Nicola.' His smile had disappeared, and his head was facing straight again. 'I'm going to garage the Rover. I'm not taking you up to your unit,' he was telling her. 'You can get there by yourself. I don't suppose there are any big bogeymen roaming the complex. I'll wait till your light goes on, but I'm not coming up to start what I know will happen. I'll wait till it's all cut and dried!'

Nicola nodded, and jumped from the Land Rover as it came to a standstill. She gazed upward at him sitting there behind the wheel. He waved her off with the flip of the hand.

She said, 'Goodnight, Drew,' and walked off.

CHAPTER TWELVE

SPILLING in from the high windows, the sunshine brought her awake next morning. Eight o'clock, well past her usual rising time, she thought, and then decided that there would be a lot of others in the same boat, after a night like last night.

Hurriedly she drank a cup of tea in the kitchen, then made her way to Reception. There were to be a lot of departures this morning, even though it was still very early. She handled bills, accepted money, smiled cheerfully, her mind completely elsewhere, until Peter lifted the flap of the counter.

'I'll take over now, Nicola,' he told her. 'I've had my breakfast. Off you go. Drew is waiting for you to go in.'

She made for the little entrance, her heartbeats quickening at the thought of the coming meeting. How would he greet her?

'That's not ours!' Peter's ejaculation came as she began to walk away. The sound of a Land Rover negotiating the ramp came clearly on the early morning air. The four-wheel-drive pulled to a stop opposite the wide open entrance doors and decanted three people out of its interior. Heartbeats suddenly a throbbing tattoo, Nicola recognised the woman stepping down from the front passenger seat to join the group already on the ground. Elspeth's was a figure to command attention. Immaculate, groomed to perfection, her raven-dark hair shone in the sunlight; her toenails flaunted the exact colour of lips and fingers. Matching slacks and a casual overblouse hid nothing of the figure beneath.

Damn, damn, damn! was the furious thought that went through Nicola's mind. Why did she have to come here, now ... today! Then the thought that she might have been invited, crossed her mind. She dropped back the flap of the counter and remained inside. All of a sudden she wasn't hungry, and didn't want to go into the dining-room.

There was no need, however, to wonder if Drew was inside still waiting for her. He stalked through and walked past the desk on his way to greet the newcomers, and all she saw was a brow as black as thunder; a stiff-backed walk giving off anger in its very bearing —he didn't glance in her direction. She heard the greeting, laughter from the woman, a male voice saying:

'God, it's a beautiful beach! I had no idea!'

Then Elspeth, coral-tipped fingers on Drew's arm was doing the introductions. It seemed the other four were from her hospital; all doctors too.

Drew raised an eyebrow in Peter's direction, and her companion passed back through the barrier. Peter gathered the party competently together and shooed them before him, Drew making up the rear.

In no time at all Peter had returned. 'Well, that's fixed that,' he commented dryly. 'Food should keep them occupied for a while. I hope to hell, however, they're only here for the day. I want to get this place cleaned up, with furniture and beds back to normal. Besides, we have that crowd of specials arriving the day after tomorrow.'

For once, Nicola wasn't concerned about the state of the resort. She made no answer. Glynis appeared through the archway and came across to them.

'Mr Huntly says you're to come to breakfast, Miss Grant.'

Nicola gave the barest suggestion of a shrug, then perforce followed Glynis back. Moving towards her own place, she gave no glance at all to the crowded tables of recent arrivals, but Drew was beside her chair before she could reach for it.

'Look, Nicola, I'm tied up with these personal guests for a few hours,' he said, and there was a decided edge to the words he was voicing. 'But I'll see you after the exodus this evening, and I tell you frankly, I'll be glad when this weekend is finally over. I've never put in one like it. Talk about things going wrong... !' Abruptly, he returned to his guests and, presumably, his own breakfast.

Herself, Nicola made a pretence of eating what Glynis set before her, and sat drinking her tea; she didn't know what to think. Wondering if Drew had meant what he had said, what he had done last night, would get her nowhere, she decided at last, and pushed back her chair to leave. She was almost at the door when she was pulled up sharply by Candace's voice, echoing from beside that crowded table by the big plate glass window.

'Oh, Nicola, here a moment!'

Nicola flipped a hand behind her in acknowledgement, but continued on her way.

'Only for a minute, Nicola,' determinedly Candace called again.

Shrugging, and because she had to, she made her way across to join the figure talking to that unexpected table of visitors.

Introducing her to the other doctors, Candace said, 'Wasn't I lucky Nicola was here, Elspeth?' and an unaccustomed nuance was in her words, the older girl beside her thought, and wondered about it, but Candace was continuing, 'Because it's through her I'm getting what I want. She was the one who persuaded Drew to see reason about my going nursing.'

Hell ... hell, what a thing to say, here and now!

What effect would such a statement have on Drew?
As if she could coax him to do anything he didn't want
to do, Nicola thought angrily. The doctor beside Elspeth saved the day; he said with a smile:

'Lucky Drew! I too could have been persuaded with
two such charming girls as you bombarding me for
permission.'

He was so disarming that Nicola smiled her own
radiant smile in return, surprising him into a more
thorough survey of her. But this time, disengaging herself from Candace's grasp, she did go on her way.

Peter being called away, Nicola found her time fully
occupied right through till after lunch. Elspeth and her
friends had gone swimming, and were now out somewhere with Drew. Gerry sauntered up to lean indolently upon her barricade.

'I'm finally off, Nicola,' he told her, producing his
slightly raffish grin. 'I begged a lift home from Elspeth,
instead of getting away this morning. I want to tell
you....' he broke off and swung round as the visiting
Land Rover pulled up before the entrance, scattering
gravel as it did so. 'I've got to go,' he continued. 'I'll
see you, though, Nicola. 'Bye for now.'

Three steps sideways to the end of her bench enabled
Nicola to have the visiting Land Rover entirely in
view. Peter—arriving back, thank goodness, she
thought—was handing up holdalls and other impedimenta. Drew was at the back of the vehicle, screened
from all sides. Elspeth went to join him. In the split
second that Nicola glanced through the big plate glass

window, the two forms had become one, locked together ... welded, Elspeth's arms clasped tightly about the man's neck. He didn't detach them. Nicola saw the embrace, the kiss, as she stood rigidly behind her enclosure.

The close-held forms disintegrated; the woman was stood apart by hands at her waist. She smiled up into the face gazing down at her, and spoke. The watcher saw that, and the laughter. Then the man bent down, kissed the face uplifted to him. They stood for a moment more, then both turned to move to the front of the vehicle.

Drew didn't come inside, he was making his way round towards his own unit. Nicola knew he had to go over to the homestead sometime today. Apparently he had decided to go now. Good! That gave her time for her own plans. She knew what she was going to do. She checked money, made out an I.O.U., put the rest back in the safe, and swung the handle. Peter wouldn't find that till long after she had left.

Sending Jim to get Peter for her, she told him when he arrived, 'Look, Peter, I want to catch the Coloured Sands bus when Mr Torrens returns with the last contigent.'

'But, Nicola....' she was interrupted.

'I have time owing to me.'

'Of course, I realise that. You can also do as you like. I know that too. But why now—and so suddenly?'

'I feel I need to get away for a few days. There's shopping I want to do in Brisbane. Everything here,' she gestured to the desk, 'is in order. You'll be able to manage until. . . .' She broke off abruptly. She wasn't going to say she wasn't coming back. Time enough for that. 'I haven't got much time, Peter. I want to pack an overnight case. Hold the bus for me, will you?'

'Yes. I'll do that, but. . . .' Distress and surprise coloured his words.

'I have to go, Peter.' Nicola turned, leaving him gazing after her retreating back, puzzlement clouding his whole countenance.

In the unit, without allowing herself time to think, she reached down her overnight case, and even in this hurrying moment, folded neatly two skirts and blouses, then crammed in all the underclothes she could manage. Scrabbling for a pair of town shoes, she noticed the afternoon dress she had bought with Naomi. This wasn't handled with care, time was running out; she shoved it in on top of the shoes and pulled at the zip. It slid half way. She was thankful for that much.

Drawing a deep breath, she took her uniform stretched it on a hanger. Fingers caressed it straight; a shrug, then it went quickly on the rod. The beautiful dress she had worn last night, when Drew had declared himself, she pushed far back in the wardrobe. She never wanted to see it again.

Pulling on the pair of jeans thrown over a chair back —an old pair, she noted, but didn't care—she slipped into a blouse and denim jacket. Into her big shoulder bag went as many cosmetics as it would hold. Glynis's voice reached her as she collected toothbrush and paste from the bathroom.

'Mr Sinclair said to tell you the bus is ready, that it's waiting for you.'

'Okay, Glynis, thanks. Tell them I'll be there in a moment.' The door closed. Nicola glanced round the room. What on earth was she doing, leaving all this? The place she loved ... the man she.... Oh, no!

A line dropped to Peter from Brisbane would return all the rest of her clothes, but not just yet. Not for a while. Not until she got herself and her feelings straightened out.

Collecting her case, and with the laden bag slung across her shoulder, she muttered to herself as she marched down the little cement path, 'Well, here I go. Brisbane, we'd better like one another!' Bypassing the office and the front entrance, she walked to where the bus waited, filled now with its complement of passengers.

'Hi, Mr Torrens,' she said, and managed to get a smile on her face. 'Any room for me?'

'There's always room for you—and if there wasn't we'd make some. Off to the big smoke for a couple of days, eh?'

'Yes, I've a few things to do, and some shopping. Where do you want me to sit?'

'Anywhere you can grab a seat. There's a couple of vacant ones.' He gave her his easygoing smile, and hoisted her overnight case up to rest beside his driving seat.

Nicola moved down the aisle. She gestured to an empty seat beside a large motherly-looking woman, and receiving a nod, dropped into it.

Down the so familiar ramp they trundled, to begin the long beach drive. The prick of tears came from behind her eyes, and hastily she groped among the purse's jumble for dark glasses. They were not used on this journey, usually, loving the view of the waves blue-green, milky-topped, crashing upon the silver sand as she did. But she put them on now, and didn't even spare a glance at the spot upon which her own place was perched.

Thanking goodness that the woman beside her was giving all her attention to the scene rushing by so swiftly outside the moving bus, and didn't appear to want to talk, Nicola turned now to the actual reason for her presence on this transport carrying her away from all she wanted.

Perhaps that first embrace could have been merely a coming together, a gesture on Elspeth's part, although it certainly had seemed passionate enough— but she had seen Drew herself, actually seen him lower his head and kiss the woman standing before him. It had been him doing the kissing, not the woman he had called a dish. She told herself for the umpteenth time, it had been Drew. And after ... after the way he had behaved when the gala dinner was over, and last night, upon the burn along the beach.

Even merely thinking of those episodes made her nerve ends quiver. And wasn't she lucky to be out of the whole mess without deeper damage? acidly the thought came. Because taking her feelings then into consideration, the emotion his mere touch brought flying, anything could have eventuated. Suddenly, the wonder came why it hadn't. Probably, and vitriol coloured this surmise, he wanted to have his altogether love scene in style—soft lights, sweet music, and champagne.

Well, thank goodness the whole drama was gone beyond recall, and temptation with it. Deliberately, Nicola turned her back on the ocean outspread before her, and faced forward. This was a new life she was embarking upon, and as they trundled through the guarding sand-dunes, she told herself she had better start making plans.

She had to get to Brisbane and find a job, but not with empty hands, she assured herself, thinking of the letters of introduction from Cairns, of the excellent references snuggled, at the bottom of the jumble resting upon her lap. She'd manage very well, thank you.

Her fare paid at Tewantin, a hand flipped in a casual farewell to the bus's complement and its driver, she made her way to the big overlander already waiting at its stop for the trip to the capital. And once on the way, driving along a different route from the one Drew had taken, she gazed out at a new countryside, and began as she meant to go on, forcing her thoughts to other things.

A last look and, satisfied, Nicola turned from the mirror, picking up her big shoulder bag. At least luck had been with her when she had reached Brisbane. Getting a room here had been fortunate. It wasn't always possible to obtain accommodation in the C.W.A. hostel, but she had belonged to the Country Women's Association in Cairns and upon stepping from a taxi two months ago had managed to snaffle lodgings here.

She had found a job, and if it could be managed she meant to remain here until deciding about a permanent home. Out now, on the pavement, she walked the few steps to the bus stop and gazed about her as always at this early hour at the pleasant prospect from up here on the high ground. Sauntering, enjoying the freshness of the morning, she looked up to break into a little run; the bus was early.

'Coming out to lunch, Nicola?' Into the austere elegance of the anteroom to the company manager's office, a head was thrust.

Nicola raised a rueful eyebrow, signing to the pile of papers beside her typewriter. 'No, I'll get Carol to bring me a cup of tea and a sandwich here, Jen,' she answered. 'The boss is at a meeting, and these have to be done for him to sign when he comes in. He leaves for Sydney at three o'clock. I'll tidy up then and leave early.'

'What are you going to do then, shop?'

'Well, not exactly. I'm going to look around to see what a unit costs ... a small one,' Nicola added, hesitating at the look on the other girl's face.

'You're lucky to be able to think of buying a unit,

Nicola. As you know, Bill and I are both saving like mad for a deposit on a house for after we're married, but even with two of us working, it won't be easy.'

'Yes ... well, I'm not going to get one right away. Look, would you like to come with me some time? I hate the thought of going on my own.'

'Gosh, I'll come like a shot! I'm happy to check all kinds of prices, but ...' Jen's voice slowed, 'not this weekend, I'm afraid. Bill's aunt is down from New Guinea and we're taking her out both Saturday and Sunday. Hey, we're going up to Lone Pine on Sunday. Would you like to come with us?'

'I couldn't intrude on visiting relatives like that. What would Bill say?'

'I don't know about Bill. I'd love you to. We wouldn't have to be thinking of things to say all the time—there'd be more of us to spread the conversation around. Please come!'

Nicola liked Jenny Smith who worked out in the main office, so with a smile she accepted the offered outing, saying, 'Thanks, Jen, I'll look forward to it.'

'About a unit—are you seriously interested in one, Nicola?' Jenny was back on a subject that was of great interest to her. 'I think that's just too marvellous.'

'It won't be right away, yet I want to get settled somewhere permanently. I have some money. Not enough for a deposit on a unit, of course, but....' Here Nicola stopped. She hated even having to mention Teewah ... or the beach. She had only now begun to stop watching for Drew's figure to loom up before her shrinking vision, sick at the thought of such a happening. Brisbane, however, was a big place, and his office could be within the radius of a mile-long street, or the crowded square of the city proper. Only an outside chance would cause them to bump into one another.

'But,' she repeated now, 'I have a little house at the seaside, a shack I expect you would call it really, that my father left me. The house isn't in itself much, but it's built on valuable land, so I'm going to put it up for sale.'

'Oh, gosh, Nicola! Lucky you! But selling a place at the seaside! Don't you want to keep it? Is it far from the ocean?'

'Actually, it's right on the sea front, right on top of the sand-dunes. You can see the water, the waves crashing down on to the shore right before your eyes.'

'You wouldn't sell that? You couldn't!'

'Yes, I could! I don't want to go there again. The only thing is that it's not a property developed beach, and it will take only a certain kind of person to want it. Still, I'm not in any rush except that I want to get settled and find something to start building my life upon.'

'What a funny thing to say, Nicola, when you are so young—that you have to start finding an interest. Why. . . .'

Shrilling a strident demand, the phone cut through the question just coming. Nicola picked it up, said, 'Yes, nearly . . . yes, I will. . . .' was silent for a minute, then again spoke into the receiver. 'Yes, I'll do it now, right away. They'll be waiting for you.

'I've got to get to work, Jen,' she said, as she put the phone down. 'I'll see you later on.' Nicola didn't even wait for the other girl's departure. She was concentrating on the papers piled beside her on the table, fingers flying with quicksilver pace over the keys of her typewriter.

Later, after tidying her desk and collecting her bag, Nicola went through into the big office and waited while Jenny, dark, competent, roly-poly figure amply compensated by a sweetness of temperament, initiated a junior into the intricacies of a legal phrase.

'About Sunday, Jen,' she asked when the latter's attention came her way, 'what are the logistics? As you know, I haven't a car. Can I get a bus to wherever....'

'We'll pick you up. It's only a short ride down to the jetty at the Quay. The river trip leaves from there. Okay?'

'Yes, very much okay. Thanks, Jen, I'll look forward to it.' Nicola flipped a hand in farewell and departed.

On Sunday morning she was in the lobby of the hostel, waiting for her transport. She glanced down ruefully at her jeans. Shabby and much washed, they were the pair which had come to her hands when she had flown from Teewah. With the same blouse, denim jacket and sandals, the whole lot comprised her getaway garb.

The outfit would pass muster, she knew that, as everyone wore anything in today's permissive fashion, but it was not normally what she herself would wear on a Sunday outing. Still, she didn't want to buy more casual gear. She would have to send for her stuff, and there was plenty of that kind among it.

She kept saying to herself that a letter must be sent to Peter—but with the qualification that later would do. Her whole metabolism shied away from anything to do with that place. She would write for it—but later.

It had taken effort even to go to the estate agent to place the beach property upon the market. But after Friday's talk with Jenny, resolutely she had marched into the one on the ground floor of their own building, putting the shack up for sale, and finally cutting any ties with Teewah.

'You realise I'll have to get someone up to inspect it for value, don't you, Miss Grant? It will be a couple of weeks before we can advertise it here in the city,' the man behind the desk had told her kindly, probably taking her reluctance for nervousness.

She had nodded, thankful it was out of her hands now. And if she had regrets about the loss of that vast splendid view, she knew also she would never go back. Drew Huntly had spoiled it for her.

Bill's car was coasting into the kerb outside, and running lightly across to it, she smiled gaily at the two in the front seat, saying, 'How do you do,' to her companion to be, in the back.

The weather was certainly turning it on for them; blue cloudless sky, golden morning, but summer was going, Nicola thought, glad of the denim jacket slung around her shoulders. As she stepped into the boat,

however, that began its chugging journey up the river
almost immediately, winter seemed far away. It was an
enchanted day, and gazing at the river banks as they
slid by, unfamiliar with this section of Brisbane, Nicola
was content. It was all a new experience with Bill making like a tourist guide both for herself and his aunt.
The large, sprawling, tree-studded stretch of ground
that was the University of Queensland's St Lucia was
pointed out, but Nicola allowed his discourse to flow
over her, just using this day as a bridge from yesterday
to tomorrow.

At Lone Pine, even the most blasé of tourists could
do nothing but fall in love with the Koalas. They were
cuddly and delightful, and all the things that were
said about them. Bill took photos. Aunt Mavis loved it
—and him, you could see. Like all the other trippers,
they lunched at the restaurant, visited the other ani-
mals, and on the launch, wending homewards, looked
back on one of life's pleasanter episodes.

Glancing round to speak to Jenny when they were
almost at the jetty, abruptly Nicola faced front again.
The two opposite her were sitting holding hands. Bill
had looked at Jenny in the exact moment Nicola had
turned. She had seen that glance, that delight in to-
getherness. Why ... why couldn't she herself have
fallen in love with an ordinary young man, got engaged and planned a future much as these two were
doing? It would have been enough.

Not now, though. She realised that. An acid smile
widened her lips at the thought of Drew sitting hold-

ing hands among a crowd of tourists on a river boat. And remembrance of the passion, the cataclysmic emotion, that had engulfed her in that same Drew Huntly's arms made the thought of any other man in her life ludicrous.

Hadn't she had proof of that only a couple of weeks ago at the office? A client, an executive, waiting for an appointment with her boss, had put a casual arm round her shoulders as she had walked over to explain. She was aware, even as she had stiffened, that no impropriety had been intended, even before he had laughed while saying, 'Don't freeze me, my dear, it's only my way.' Abruptly, she had smiled, the warmth of her expression radiating out to him. 'I know,' she explained. 'It was just that I remembered something,' and ushered him forward as the intercom squawked.

A cool breeze heralding the evening swept across the wide stretch of water, Nicola shivered suddenly. It didn't do to look back on memories. She pushed her arms entirely into the jacket's sleeves and stood up. They were coming to journey's end.

CHAPTER THIRTEEN

IT was on the following Friday when she was tidying her desk, preparing to leave for the day, that her phone rang. Answering it, she was surprised that it was herself being enquired for.

'Yes, speaking,' she replied into the receiver.

'I've had a man from our country office out to appraise your property, Miss Grant.'

'Thank you, Mr Dexter. What did he say?'

'He said he liked it, that you would have no trouble selling it. It's becoming quite fashionable to get away from it all these days, as you no doubt know. He did say you might have to wait a little until the right buyer comes along. He has no doubts about you being able to dispose of it, however. Around seventeen thousand dollars, he thought. How will that suit you, Miss Grant?'

'You're not joking, are you?'

'I never joke about business Miss Grant. Our agent has put up a "For Sale" notice upon it, and if that doesn't bring results, we'll advertise it. Will that be all right?'

'Yes....' the words came slowly. Then, 'Yes, thank you, Mr Dexter.'

'Very well. Call in next week to have a little chat about it. Goodbye.'

Nicola heard the phone go down, but her own receiver remained glued to her hand. Eventually replacing it, she walked slowly out through the main office as if sleepwalking.

'Hi, Nicola, hang on a moment. I'll go down with you.' Jenny swung round to head for the hallway by her side, and as the elevator door closed behind them, asked sharply, after a glance at her friend's face, 'What's the matter, Nicola?'

'Nothing. Are you in a hurry? Can you spare the time to have a milk shake with me?'

Jenny nodded, saying no more, and with other chatting employees they took the lift to the ground floor. Out on busy Queen Street, moving with, and against, the hurrying stream of toilers freed for home-going or the pleasures of the coming evening, they walked the hundred yards to turn into the open aperture that was the milk bar. Clutching their large cardboard containers after being served, they edged their way to a corner table.

Relating what Mr Dexter had just told her, Nicola added, 'I can't believe it, Jen. It's so much more than I'd expected.'

'But isn't it wonderful for you, Nicola? Lucky thing that you are!' There was not the slightest sign of envy in the last remark, only the warmth of congratulations.

'Yes, I expect it is. But there's a saying, isn't there, that you win one, you lose one. I'm not all that lucky.

Still, I'll get my unit now, and as I told you once before, begin to make a life for myself.'

'You know, Nicola, you're funny. You're not twenty-one yet, and you talk as if you had no marvellous happenings waiting around the corner for you. We'll have to start taking you around to our parties, and tennis do's. . . .'

'No!' the interruption came abruptly. Then, softening her reply, Nicola continued, 'No, but thanks, Jen. I don't want to go to any parties; not yet anyway. Maybe later.' There—there was her catchcry again. 'I only. . . .' She saw the raised eyebrow and the look on the face of the girl opposite.

She continued, but reluctantly, words dragging, 'I'm not interested in meeting men, which is what you intend. I . . . I liked a man once, very much, but nothing came of it. I don't want to get involved again—at least, not at this moment—perhaps later.'

Later! And the way she felt now, it would be a long time later. 'Look,' she said, changing the subject, 'I feel like splurging. Mr Dexter was so definite, he insists there'll be no trouble about my sale, so let's go and do the town tomorrow night. You've been so good to me, you and Bill. I'd like to return some of it. We'll have dinner somewhere nice and expensive to celebrate.'

'I'll ask Bill and phone you, if that's what you really want?'

'It's exactly what I want. Okay then, phone me in the morning and I'll book us in somewhere.' A glance at the time caused her to exclaim, 'Hell, I've missed one bus! I'd better get the next one or I'll be walking home. You've got plenty of trains running, you're okay, but I've only got a couple of buses. See you!' Nicola waved and turned—a young girl, thinner now than the day she had arrived in the south, long shining blonde hair swinging about her shoulders, blue eyes searching her way to the bus stop. One of the hundreds of women in that particular region, at that particular time of day.

Next morning she set about her Saturday tasks; washed clothes, shampooed and set her hair, creamed all the skin she could reach, removed old polish and re-did the new, on both fingernails and toes. She folded the dry clothes before lunch, which she decided to give a miss, and curled up on her bed with a book. It remained unopened.

She had resolved to write to Peter today about her other clothes, but she knew she wouldn't. How long would it take her to wipe the Teewah affair from her mind? Oh, she was sleeping better at long last, but thinking of Drew was something she tried to limit.

How was she going to go on? The old cliché said time heals all things, and she accepted that. But how much did it take? Time would have to be made friends with. And this book lying there waiting to waft her to other scenes could be used for that purpose. Determinedly, she picked it up.

Reading until it was time to shower and dress, Nicola took from its hanger the afternoon dress Naomi had salesmanshipped her into. Nothing like 'The Dress' she never wanted to see again; yet its brown glow lifted the blue of her eyes and brought out the golden lights from newly washed hair. Lipsticked and perfumed, she decided she would do, and catching up her handbag—her evening purse was probably lying in a suitcase somewhere—flipped the switch and closed the door.

Lights, the hurrying movement of vehicles, the crowded pavements along the theatre side of Queen Street, brought their own brand of enjoyment, and suddenly Nicola was glad she had suggested this outing. They strolled, window-gazed, placidly content with each other's company. She was not even aware of a car swishing much too quickly up the side of the street upon which they walked, of a sudden braking, of an expert backing into a very small space at the kerb.

Her heart jolted. Candace's voice, carrying across to them as she stepped from out the low door, brought her to an abrupt standstill. For a moment, she was absolutely unable to move, then she had turned to the large plate-glass window beside her, unaware of any of its contents. She hadn't realised she was holding her breath, until it exhaled, unable to be held any longer. They had moved, Candace and Gerry, away from their vicinity, down towards a theatre entrance. But in that brief heart-stopping unexpected encounter, Nicola had felt the world spin.

It showed her, if she had thought she was getting over Drew, how wrong she had been. For his sister's voice to be able to do what it had done to her!

Making herself give the impression of enjoying the dinner, exquisitely cooked and presented, she thought the others noted nothing different. But she could have been eating dust and ashes.

'Hey, Nicola, ready to leave?' Jenny's head poked round the door as Nicola was putting the cover over her typewriter.

'Yes, coming now.' A swift assessing glance round the room, the collection of her bag, and she joined Jenny, closing the door behind her.

'Have you heard from the estate firm yet, Nicola?' her companion asked as they descended in the lift.

'No. I really don't expect to for a while. They only appraised it and put up the sign on Friday. And it's only Tuesday today, you know. How is Bill's Aunt Mavis, Jenny? She goes back to New Guinea this week, doesn't she?'

'Yes, for two more years, then they're coming back to Australia to live. She's really nice, isn't she? I'm glad I like her, because they dote on one another.'

'That showed the other day. But Bill is a nice man, as you said to me once. You're lucky, Jen.'

'Yes, he is, and I am. He said to say thanks for a super dinner last Saturday. He also said we must do it again.'

Waiting for the bus at her stop, Nicola turned to phrase her next sentences to show only what the words meant. 'It was pleasant, but I think, Jen, I'd rather go on excursions like the one we did to Lone Pine. I really enjoyed that. I'd like to go to Sea World, and across to the island to Tangalooma, and all those other places I've never been to. I'd like to see some of the places around our own city.'

It wasn't, she knew, the actual wanting to go to these unexplored spots, although she'd be quite happy for the chance to see them. She wanted no more shocks such as bumping into anyone from her life of a couple of months ago. Candace and Gerry would hardly be on such trips as she had proposed, especially Gerry. He had his own transport, and his own way of doing things—like Drew.

'Look, Jen, here's my bus. See you tomorrow and we'll discuss it some more, eh?' Waving goodbye, Nicola took her turn up the steps.

As the bus pulled up a hundred yards or so from the hostel, she moved down the aisle. The two steps were negotiated, and Nicola strolled homewards, enjoying the gentleness of the early evening. Twilight wasn't upon the city yet, but the sun was on its way to rest for the night. Past a car stationary at the kerb, its door swinging wide, she walked, hardly noticing it.

Shock, at an arm being grabbed and the momentum generated with the shove that sent her sprawling in an awkward bundle across the front seat, came flying. Then she straightened, more furious than frightened. But the car had swished forward, its engine having already been murmuring as it stood waiting.

'You needn't try to open the door and fall out, as they do in all good storybooks, either,' Drew's voice told her. 'This is not any old car, and that door is locked until opened by a key.'

Anger blazed, staining her furious retort. 'What a thing to do! Are you mad? Turn round and take me home at once, do you hear?' Her voice rose as the car continued on without the slightest deviation.

The driver took his glance from the road for the briefest moment, and meeting that look directed at her, Nicola went silent. The face that had swung her way seemed so different from the one in her memory. Oh, no, it wasn't, though. She had seen it like that once before, when he had believed she had just come out of Gerry's room.

She turned, gazing out of her window at the stream of homegoing cars. What could she do? Any healthy, determined young girl wouldn't sit here calmly, her subconscious was telling her. But what was the alternative? She was in no doubt that the door was locked, as Drew had informed her it was. To try to get hold of the wheel could cause not only an accident to themselves, with vehicles streaming along on both sides, but to others too. Besides, even if that profile seemed chiselled out of granite, when it came down to basics, she would be taken home. This was Drew!

She settled back, gazing straight before her.

'That's being sensible,' said the hateful voice. 'Now, put your seat belt on. I don't want the police pulling me up at this particular moment.' He was fumbling with his own, which, with that rocketing take-off, he had been unable to spare attention for.

Nicola made no attempt to fasten hers. What did

she care if they were in an accident, or if they were pulled up for a breach of the Traffic Act?

A chuckle wafted towards her stiff figure. 'I'm not going to risk the slightest thing that could cause even the smallest accident, if that's what you're wishing on me. This will be one of the most careful drives of my life, I assure you.'

No reply was vouchsafed; her gaze turned disdainfully away. She didn't recognise the section of the city they were driving through, and although there were still streams of cars, they were thinning. Apparently they were edging more into the outer suburbs. Unable to prevent herself, she asked, 'Where are you taking me?'

'Home!'

Her voice went high as it had at the beginning of this bizarre affair. 'Home? You really are mad, Drew!' Then, without noticing the entreaty her words carried, she added, 'Please take me back. You're going to have to, anyway—I'll be missed. They'll be wondering where I've got to and report it, and you won't like that. The great Drew Huntly mixed up in a silly scandal!'

'Oh, you do remember my name! I wondered! And no one will miss you. There'll be a phone call explaining your absence ... tonight! Also one to your office tomorrow....'

He broke off as she interjected, 'What do you mean, my absence tonight, and my office tomorrow? You really are mad! Why have you done this stupid, senseless thing?'

'I have a reason I think good and proper.'

'You might think you have. I have just as good and proper a reason for being taken home. And I'm going. Don't think you can keep me anywhere against my will. The days of white slavery have gone. Fancy abducting a girl from a city street!' She came up again with her catch-cry. 'You've gone mad!'

'And even if you phone the office, they won't believe you. They won't believe I left without a moment's notice—without telling anyone.'

'But you have done just that very thing before, haven't you? Left at a moment's notice—and told no one.'

The voice that spoke those words had dropped to a degree of chill unheard-of. Nicola didn't know how to answer it, to answer this inimical presence. She couldn't say, imitating his words, that on that occasion she too had had what she thought a good and proper reason for her behaviour. She sat back, and finding her hands shaking, clasped them tightly in her lap.

A sharp turn and they were swinging off the highway into a side street. The grounds of the houses were much more spacious here than those of the inner city. It was more than twilight now. Dusk was with them, and darkness was closing in. Would she have a chance to run when he stopped the car?—and then, suddenly, she decided how silly she was being. She muttered, 'This is Drew, this isn't some film gangster.' They would have a talk, and when he had had his say, he would take her home.

Another sharp turn, and the Jaguar had swung into a driveway. Nicola had a glimpse of a low white house with arches, and then a garage door rolled up silently, opened perhaps by a gadget from within the car itself. It would be, she thought scornfully, just the contrivance Drew would make use of. And behind them the door had shut just as silently. The barely heard engine echoed all around, and headlights flung back their brilliance from the wall before them. The driver slid from the car, holding the door wide.

'Out,' he said.

When she made no attempt to comply, he told her, 'Get out, Nicola. Or do you want me to carry you?' For the first time she realised he had spoken her name.

Moving across the seat to the driving door entrance, she had to manoeuvre awkwardly over the gear panel and under the wheel. Drew made no attempt to help her at all. When finally she was out, he reached across to switch off the headlamps and close the door.

Hand on her elbow, he piloted her across the echoing room and she heard a key turn. Then light in its brightness brought her hand up to shade her eyes. Through a doorway which Drew shut, and locked, behind them, asking, 'Do you know what a deadlock is, Nicola?'

She shook her head.

'A deadlock,' he began, as if starting a lecture, 'locks both ways. You lock it from the inside too, and it needs a key to unlock it to get out.'

Nicola didn't understand what he was talking about;

actually she wasn't trying to understand. All this guff about locks—what did she care?

Her companion threw out a hand to the space about them, replying grimly in answer to the blank look she was directing at him. 'I'm only trying to explain that you just can't walk up to a door and open it to leave. You need these.' He jiggled a bunch of keys. 'As I have a great deal of valuable stuff here and am away a lot—which you no doubt know—I try to protect it. So although these locks were not installed for this little episode, they've come in very handy for it.' He lifted an eyebrow, apparently courting her reply.

She didn't answer him, just stood gazing around, dazed a little, upset a lot. What did she care—at least at this particular moment—about him and his damn locks?

'Pay a little more attention to me, Nicola. I don't think you've understood what it's all about. Because, besides the doors, every window has its ornamental scroll which doubles for bars. Oh, nothing so vulgar as the prison variety. Still, they take the place of them: and they protect this house very well—as they should! I designed the place myself. So get it into your head that you're here in it to stay, and you're not getting out.'

They were standing on tiles; unlike any she had ever seen before. Now he guided her down two steps into what was a huge living room; tiled as well, these were different from those covering the hallway—coloured, vivid, beautiful. High white walls and ceilings, broken only with symmetrical archways, added to the impression of old Spain—or, Nicola's lips twisted wryly, a Moorish palace. Especially the latter, she thought, after taking in the low tables, shining brass, ivory inlaid, carved and polished, standing beside fat ottomans scattered about the spaciousness of the room.

Drew was watching, silent now, as she glanced about her; her gaze pausing on the two pictures the walls held —in what was almost an austere chamber. The Namatjira was smaller than the one at Teewah, but its colours glowed against the plainness of its surroundings. She gave to it all the admiration it deserved—and only a single glance in passing to its partner on the opposite wall, unknowing if it was impressionist, abstract, or whatever.... It was then that she saw Drew's expression.

'You don't like it, Nicola?' he asked, and he was back to looking like the ordinary Drew she had sometimes known; amusement sounding in his voice.

Nicola shrugged. 'To me it's like throwing paint haphazardly on to a canvas and then allowing it to dry where it will. But of course, what does it matter what an uneducated peasant thinks?'

'Yes, well....' he laughed. 'More than the Namatjira,' he said, 'that picture is most of the reason for all the security. Still, I didn't realise when I installed it how handy it was to become for this little caper.'

His tone had changed again, and she stared helplessly at him. His expression as well as his voice took on a new look. 'I think a bath and a change of clothing would do something for you, Nicola. You give the impression of being a bit draggled, as if you'd put in a long hard day. I'll show you to your room and a bathroom, shall I?'

'Oh ... oh ... you... !' Who had coined that overworked phrase? but it did fit this scene, it *did*. Anyone to use those words to her *was* a male chauvinist pig. She glared at him, hate filling her glance. From the spotless cream cashmere rollnecked sweater to the lightest of fawn slacks, he was immaculate, and this minute she hated him more for his remark about her crumpled appearance than that he had abducted and ill-used her.

'I don't want any bath! I'm not staying here!' Her answer came coated with ice.

'Oh, but you are, you know.'

They stood yards opposite one another, he, with eyes half shut, smiling a smile Nicola didn't like, she glaring.

'Also, might I dare to add, I like my women fresh and clean, and perfume-sprayed, when I make love to them.'

'Bully for you! Isn't it a shame one of your women isn't here right now?'

'Oh, I think she is. And there's time for the perfume spraying and what have you—all night, actually.'

Nicola gestured helplessly. 'Please, Drew,' she begged, 'isn't it time we put an end to this verbal sparring? I really am not staying, you know.'

'How are you going to leave? And like it or not—

and allow me to express the hope that it will be the former—I'm going to make love to you. I've been looking forward to this moment for two long months, and there's no way you are going to deprive me of it.'

Actually, for the first time, she began to really take this bizarre happening seriously. Before, she had thought, this is Drew. It doesn't matter how he acts, or what he says, I know him. I've lived in the same complex all those months in his company. He's made love to me, and although I've fallen fathoms deep, head over heels in love with him, and he knows it; that's where it stopped. This is just an act he's putting on.

But it wasn't an act any more. He meant it. She looked at the ruthless face opposite and saw no sign of softening. Her back stiffened, and searching for words, she said baldly.

'What satisfaction would you get out of such love-making? I wouldn't be involved in it at all, but I wouldn't fight it. I wouldn't demean myself doing something so undignified.'

'I'll get satisfaction all right!'

God, she thought, that's his silken tone, the one he only uses when he wants something and means to get it, come hell or high water. It shouldn't be used now.

'And I think . . .' he was continuing, still in that voice 'you'll find yourself involved.'

'I won't! And even if I did, when this episode of,' her lip curled, 'what used to be called a fate worse than death is over, I'll walk out of here. It won't matter to me. I've already accepted that I won't ever want to get married; won't ever want to be involved with any man again. You've cured me of that!

'But I will make my own life. I can now. I've got enough money to start doing that very thing. Oh, nothing like this,' a disparaging arm gestured around at the big, lovely room, 'but enough for what will suit me.'

'All of seventeen thousand dollars' worth.' The words hit her and she gasped.

CHAPTER FOURTEEN

'How did you know?'

'How did you think I found you? I bought your place at Teewah on Saturday—on a condition; the condition being knowledge of whom I was buying it from, and their address.'

'You've bought my father's place?' All his other words hadn't registered.

'Yes!'

Drew watched her, then spoke again. 'I was only given your office address as that was the one you supplied to the estate agent. But, to use a gangster's idiom, casing the joint over the weekend, I realised a busy city street was no place to persuade you to come with me. So it was a case of finding out where you lived, and how you got home, which I did yesterday ... and hey presto!'

'Persuade?' she said bitterly.

'You could call it that. Look, Nicola, why don't you take me up on that bath and change? You said yourself you could walk away from this. So let's have dinner in a civilised manner, and then take it from there.'

The girl he had called Nicola so casually gazed at him. What else was there to do? She nodded. He walked past her across this beautiful room, up into the hallway and down a corridor with the blood-red tiles, to open a door. This room, however, was carpeted, and the figure before her walked across it, gesturing to a dressing table as he went. He eased back a sliding door into a wardrobe. She saw her clothes hanging there, and no doubt, the thought came tartly, the dressing table would hold the rest of her stuff.

'Yes,' he answered her look, 'they've been here since you ran away and left no forwarding address. Why in hell did you do it after.... No!' He answered his own question. 'We'll go into all that after we eat. Now, what about wearing that blue-green thing you wore at the gala dinner? It should bring back memories.' His eyebrow sky high, he walked out and closed the door.

A dressing gown was dragged from its hanger, but 'the blue-green thing' was shoved to the back of the wardrobe. There was no way in the world that it was going to be worn. Finding the bathroom, already pointed out, Nicola discovered there was no lock on this door. Probably taken off—for this caper, she muttered, using his words. Searching for a chair to push under the knob, she found only a fancy iron-work affair, but a huge powder-puff saved the day, making a wedge between its rounded back and the doorknob. 'There,' she told the powder-puff, 'stay put!'

And yes, they were barred—the windows. Even here in the bathroom the delicate-seeming scrollwork was in evidence. Nicola turned her back on them. Moving towards the shower recess, abruptly she flung away, as memory of words just spoken, came crowding. Damn him, again came the thought. She put the plug in the bathtub and quickly flipped on the taps.

Deliberately then she rummaged through the glass-stoppered bottles outspread upon a vanity table in the annex. Finding one, the fragrance of which appealed to her, she tipped half of it into the steadily rising water. 'He'll be able to smell perfume tonight!' the utterance came accompanied with smiling malice.

She lay in the water completely covered with froth. Eventually, thinking she might have a visitor if she stayed here much longer, she stepped from the bubbling, frothy, expensive-smelling water. As she sniffed, a grin formed. A fragrance was certainly wafting about her. Whether it would please was another matter.

She slipped on an apricot-coloured crêpe-de-chine dress that fell straight from her shoulders, stepped into high-heeled white sandals, whose acquaintance she was glad to renew; a last comb of hair that fell shining about her shoulders, and she was ready. A needful deep breath was inhaled, and the big living room received her.

'God!' Moving from the kitchen to place a covered dish upon the dining room table, Drew stopped, quite suddenly. He said again, 'God, but you look lovely. When you do do something, you certainly do it with a vengeance—did I say something like that on another occasion? I think I remember some words about an ice maiden.'

I'm not going to blush. I'm not! Nicola walked the two steps up to the dining room to stand against the bar between it and the kitchen. Drew poured sherry into a crystal glass and handed it across. His smile went wider at her slowness at accepting it. 'Me too,' he said, and poured a second glass to the brim. They drank it slowly while he went about his business in the small compact enclosure.

'Only a steak and salad, I'm afraid,' he told her, preparing to take the meal through to the dining room. 'I'm not one of those characters you hear about who can turn their hands to anything. My lady!' He performed a bow that a cavalier would not have been ashamed of, as he pulled out her chair.

They ate in mostly silence, Nicola not knowing what subject to bring up, Drew apparently satisfied to just eat his food. They had eaten together hundreds of times; this was no different, she was telling herself. But she knew that it was. At least she could gaze around and pretend an interest in the charming room.

Finished himself, Drew stood to collect her pushed-away plate. 'No, stay there,' he told her, as she made to rise, and returning he plonked down a platter.

'Oh,' said Nicola. It contained a Bombe Alaska.

'I heard you and Candace complaining to Peter about meanness from some management executives,' he shrugged in explanation for its presence. 'So. . . .' Drew was continuing as he cut the largest size piece her plate would hold, and passed it over, 'here's your share now.'

They had too, Candace and she, Nicola remembered; but it had been only in fun that they had been rubbishing Peter about never getting their dinner. Drew had now set the dessert aside and was pouring coffee into the cups already set waiting for it.

'Aren't you going to have some?' Nicola spoke naturally, as if asking an ordinary question to an ordinary man; but his eyelids went down, shading his eyes.

'God, no! That muck! What do you take me for? I'll have some cheese, and,' a second time he rose, 'a brandy with my coffee. Shall I pour one for you?' He held aloft a cognac bottle.

'No, thank you. That muck!' she replied in much the same tone he had used. 'You stay with your muck and I'll stay with mine. I'm going to eat this slowly, because I shan't possibly have room for another slice.'

A shout of laughter brought lightness into the brittle atmosphere, and Nicola looked at him. He was gazing directly at her, his eyes smiling. Her glance dropped.

The meal was finished with practically no more conversation, Nicola eating through the slushy concoction upon her plate, Drew drinking his coffee and swirling his brandy around his glass between sips.

As she placed her spoon upon an empty plate, he drained both his glass and small cup in two swift movements. 'I'll just take these dishes into the kitchen,' he explained, rising. Nicola pushed back her chair too and began to collect crockery. Stacked into the dishwasher, it was switched on, then a different Drew from the dinnertime one was turning to her.

'Now,' he began, 'we'll go into the lounge and I'll learn why you walked away from me without a single word!'

As she stood rooted to the floor at the change of tone, an arm came out to help her onwards. On a long, spacious ottoman, Drew turned a little sideways to face her. Their knees touching, a hand behind her shoulders, he spoke one word. 'Why?'

'I saw you. You and Elspeth ... kissing behind the Land Rover. I wasn't ... I'm not stupid.... I knew that you liked her, that you'd been involved together in a more than friendly affair; that it could have been her offering the kisses. But ... but after you moved apart from what looked like a torrid embrace ...' her glance swung swiftly up to that impassive face inches away, then quickly down to her fingers plaiting in her lap, 'she, Elspeth, looked up at you half laughing and spoke. You—it was *you*, Drew, who put your hands at her waist and bent down to kiss her. It wasn't her, it was you. And ... only the evening before....'

'Oh, God!' The exclamation echoed around them. 'I did, didn't I! Hell and damnation! Such a little thing to cause all the uproar it did. That kiss of mine, my dear Nicola, was only a farewell gesture, to thank Elspeth for making the ending so painless. She had a pretty good idea of how things stood and was already viewing new pastures. But I think ...' amusement showed for a brief second, 'she just wanted to make sure it was all over, hence the first passionate interlude.'

'It wasn't a little thing to me. I know I'm not beautiful, or eyecatching, or rich as Elspeth is, and no doubt a dozen others you could find among the circle you move in. But I have my own values. I'm good at what I do. I realise, though, that where you're concerned I'm not rational. And on the beach when you were speaking about our future, you never once mentioned marriage.' The man beside her moved restlessly, but she continued on, taking no notice. 'So, seeing you and Elspeth behind the Land Rover, and knowing the way I feel about you, I decided not to be just one of a string in your ongoing affairs. I left!'

She was pulled close against him. Her whole body stiffened, but it availed her nothing. Drew was kissing her; his lips travelling down from cheek-line to throat, to remain. Nicola could feel them through every pulse her body was taking, could feel her own heartbeat jolt. Then they had moved and had claimed her lips; and any resistance she had formed, any decisions she might have made, were gone beyond recall. And she didn't care. This emotion, this experience, was worth anything it would cost in time to come.

Her body arched to meet the one holding her; she felt his lips lift as he spoke, but she didn't want to hear. The sliding movement of crêpe-de-chine as his hands slipped upon it vanished into the mists of time, and on the ottoman, lying where he had eased her, the thud of his heartbeats overflowed all other sensations; his closeness was all that mattered. Then, abruptly, his body had moved. Her eyes, opening, looked dazedly into those of slate-grey, darkened with passion, and she moved further into the curves of a torso that was familiar, wanted. She didn't need to talk. She wanted Drew and what came of this experience.

'No!' The single word flowed through the curtain of warmth and desire that was the only encirclement Nicola was aware of. She ignored it, turning her face upwards to meet his kisses.

'No!' The exclamation came again. Drew was off the ottoman, and standing, was pulling her upright. Almost unaware of her actions, her own eyes too, like the ones she was gazing into, showed dark, shadowed, as her hand went out to him in entreaty.

'Look, Nicola, wait! I meant to be sensible; only to get our affairs straightened out of whatever I might have frightened you with earlier. I thought, too, I had some control. I didn't expect one kiss would lead to this, and if we keep on in the direction we are going, it can only end up in one way. You realise that?'

'I don't care!'

'But I do! And if you don't care now, you might later. As far as you know you could still be one of the many strings to my bow. Wasn't that what you said?'

She winced. 'Yes, I did. I still don't care.'

The man didn't wince; he drew in his breath sharply. 'You're not much bloody help, Nicola. Especially as speaking like this; acting like this, is just not my scene. I'm much more likely to take all that's offered. But with us, we had something different, and I wanted to keep it that way. That was what made me so wild when you sloped off—and in the way you did. When I finally found you—and I always would have, one way or another—I thought up this caper to get what I thought was my own back for two long miserable months of not knowing where you were.

'Even so,' the tense, hurrying voice, was continuing, 'the outcome of tonight's little session on that,' a hand gestured downwards, 'could have swung either way after it started and got out of hand. But I'm sober and sensible now, so why don't we sit down and make plans? You in your chair, and I in mine.' He wasn't laughing as he said it, either.

Not wanting to move away from him for even those few yards, Nicola yet did as she was bid, because she had no choice, and listened politely as he continued.

'You'll give your notice in the proper way. I'm known here and I don't want you disappearing, then turning up married to me. Oh, and one other thing I'll be thankful for at long last. I won't have Candace behaving to me as if I were a monster from outer space. Someone must have been to blame for your leaving, and who but me fitted the picture, was all she would say every time we met. Well, she'll have something else to occupy her the next time. Wedding plans.

'So now, how about bed?' he finished. 'It's been a long day—one I wouldn't care to go through again.'

'All right, Drew, but I haven't seen all over the house yet. Can I see the rest of it now?' Innocence personified was in the question.

The look he threw her way suddenly changed the atmosphere about them. 'No!' and the answer was brusque. 'You damn well can't. I don't want you anywhere near my room. Come on, I'll see you to yours ... *now*!'

Nicola had no say. Her arm was gripped in no lover's clasp, and the corridor echoed with the noise of her high heels as they tapped along it. Her companion must have been wearing loafers, for no sound came from them.

At her door, she turned naturally into his embrace, her cheek against the cashmere sweater, against the heartbeats that told their own story.

With the briefest of hesitation, Drew's arms enfolded her, his kiss giving all the reassurance needed. Nicola's arms reached up to clasp behind his neck, she stretched her body to melt into the one so very close. It lasted a minute, an eternity ... the ecstasy; then it was over. Drew had gone, just like that, leaving her standing outside her closed door.

Only a remark from across his departing back came echoing. 'I'll see you in the morning, Nicola. Goodnight!'

Harlequin Plus
THE LANGUAGE OF DOWN UNDER

"It's a piece of cake! Any dude could handle it."

A city person on a horse about to tackle a slice of birthday cake? Of course not. Merely a statement that a certain task is easy and that anyone can perform it. The above is an example of common American slang, and while it may be perfectly clear to us what the speaker is saying, the meaning might well be lost on a person from some other English-speaking country—such as Australia. Not to be outdone, however, the Australians have a few for us.

Australian salute (the act of brushing away flies)

to bag (to disparage)

Black Stump (imaginary last post of civilization)

a galah (a nincompoop)

a greasy (a cook for a bunch of men)

grog (alcohol, usually beer)

grey meanie (parking policeman)

to be on someone's hammer (to pick on or persecute someone)

illywhacker (professional trickster, con man)

to jerry to (to catch on)

kangaroos in one's top paddock (crazy)

to put the mockers on (to destroy one's plans)

the rabbit proof (the fence marking borders between certain Australian states)

wallaper (policeman)

warby (a disreputable-looking person)

FREE!

A hardcover Romance Treasury volume containing 3 treasured works of romance by 3 outstanding Harlequin authors...

...as your introduction to Harlequin's Romance Treasury subscription plan!

Romance Treasury

...almost 600 pages of exciting romance reading every month at the low cost of $6.97 a volume!

A wonderful way to collect many of Harlequin's most beautiful love stories, all originally published in the late '60s and early '70s. Each value-packed volume, bound in a distinctive gold-embossed leatherette case and wrapped in a colorfully illustrated dust jacket, contains...
- 3 full-length novels by 3 world-famous authors of romance fiction
- a unique illustration for every novel
- the elegant touch of a delicate bound-in ribbon bookmark... and much, much more!

Romance Treasury

...for a library of romance you'll treasure forever!

Complete and mail today the FREE gift certificate and subscription reservation on the following page.